IN THE MIDDLE OF NOWHERE

IN THE MIDDLE OF NOWHERE

A NOVEL BY

FANNY HOWE

NEW YORK

FICTION COLLECTIVE

For C.B.

First Edition

Library of Congress Cataloging in Publication Data

Howe, Fanny.
   In the middle of nowhere.

   I. Title.
PS3558.089I5   1983   813'.54   83-16540
ISBN 0-914590-82-0
ISBNo-914590-83-9 (pbk.)

Published by the Fiction Collective with assistance from the National Endowment for the Arts and the New York State Council on the Arts.

Grateful acknowledgement is also made for the support of Brooklyn College and Teachers & Writers Collaborative.

Typeset by Open Studio, Ltd., in Rhinebeck, New York, a non- profit facility for writers, artists and independent literary publishers, supported in part by grants from the New York State Council on the Arts.

Manufactured in the United States of America.

Text design: McPherson & Company
Cover design: Colleen McCallion
Author photograph: Elaine Emmanuel

The nature of God is a circle of which the center is everywhere and the circumference is nowhere.

Origin Unknown

ONE

Just before noon, there was a little bang and, weeping, the man fell dead.

His wife was dropping bread into her supermarket basket.

His daughter was in line for lunch at school.

His secretary was in the parish house, unpeeling a banana.

And no one noticed that the bells struck thirteen times that day, an uncanny slip on the part of the bell ringer, who didn't know the Rector was dead and remained terrified of his wrath for several hours.

The girl leaned out the window with a sensation of dread. It was like the statement, "There is no door." She breathed heavily, as if the outer air were a liquor which could soothe her anxiety. And it did make her smile. She leaned inside again.

She was seventeen. Her room was the room of a person that age. There were wild attempts at style, undermined by sloth. Wall hangings, beads hanging, books on the floor, a thrift shop quilt made out of old kitchen towels, and make-up littering a childish white vanity table with ripped white lacing.

This was Kathy, the lead singer in the church choir. She never sang outside the church, though her voice was bold and golden. She was a long tall white girl with long straight brown hair, brown eyes, a long neck, and a thrusting posture. Her gestures were gawking, awkward. She had humor in her heart-shaped puckered lips, but her eyes were farouche, like a nervous deer. Even alone. She bashed, rather than moved, her way through space.

Cursing often. All she wanted, she told her mother, was time to think. She had no ambition, and graduation was only months away. Her mother fretted over this fact, but couldn't dream up a solution. Kathy was, in any case, immovable, beyond the sphere of human influence. She was still a virgin, by choice, and believed in an intelligent Creator, seriously. But she swore like a sailor, and sprawled in a boyish fashion, making mean remarks about this and that. As if she were two-in-one.

The only person Kathy really loved was her mother. The rest was confusing. Her father had run off with another woman, and the woman he chose ended up as Kathy's stepfather's sister. Kathy's stepfather, Randy, was a short and husky man who ran the construction company Kathy's father used to drive a truck for. Randy's first wife had run off with a black foreman, and when Randy's sister ran off with Randy's father, Randy came to

court and comfort Kathy's mother, saying, "It's in the cards."
"And you're the card," was Kathy's response to that. She didn't
like her stepfather and his two sons. But there they were, forced
on her, night and day, because of her mother's dread of solitude.

Kathy also disliked the little town they all lived in, north of
Providence, in the middle of nowhere. Ashville consisted of a
few small farms, vegetable stands, and a village green bordered
by a small shopping area, two churches, and the library. The
weather was the only entertainment.

There was also a class division in Ashville, of which Kathy was
acutely conscious. It lay between those who had lived there for a
century, or more, and the newcomers, like herself, who lived in a
condominium settlement on the edge of town. The only place
where both classes met in peace was in the church. The
economic needs of the church made class attitudes untenable.
Kathy, always curious about human hypocrisy, could barely
stomach the Ashville congregation.

Now, staring out the window, she almost wished there were no
people on earth, but just floating consciousness. She liked the
look of nature — sudden streams in the deep woods, a strand of
ice on a brown bush, a forgotten apple freezing on a branch,
roses blackening on a fence — but she couldn't stare forever. She
had a blind date.

✣

Her blind date was named Elmer. He appeared at eight-fifteen. Kathy's mother came out to look him over in the hall.

Hello, Elmer.

How do you do, Ma'am.

Don't make it too late.

No, Ma'am.

Kathy noticed her Mom's response to Elmer before she noticed her own. It was not negative, but held some suspicion. He was older than the usual High School dates, probably close to twenty. Kathy had been told he didn't smoke or drink and worked as an automechanic in town. He was said to be cute, and straight. In a glance the description fit.

Outside, in the chill, Kathy followed him to his car, a '66 Mustang in pretty good condition. Elmer jingled his keys watching her let herself in. He wore tight levis, a checkered shirt, suede desert boots and a dark corduroy jacket. Must be about six feet, well built, shaggy blond hair. She felt him looking her over and locked herself in the car.

I don't really dig these dances, he said.

I don't either, but it's all there is.

In these parts, true.

You don't come from around here?

No way. The southwest.

Why did you come to Ashville?

Long story.

Oh.

They drove on down the dim streets. Alot of near-bare trees, yellow windows, but no streetlights. The high school was up on a hill behind an apple orchard. People from congested areas came out in the fall to pick baskets of apples — several pounds for a few bucks — off those now-empty trees. Once Kathy worked at the orchard, weighing the apples for the people. She told Elmer this as he turned up towards the school.

You got a social security number? he asked.

Just got it, she said.
     Sometimes I gross three hundred a week.
No shit.

     Yeah and the boss keeps giving me more work.
You like that?
     Sure, I put it in savings.
What are you saving for?
     I dunno, really, but I will, when I do.
That's the thing about money, said Kathy.

They were on their way to a High School dance which turned
out to be a bore. Hardly anyone showed up. The band was
playing loud and toneless hard rock. The smell of marijuana
was pungent in the green gym. Kathy was wearing a green
polyester shirt with grey swirls, fake paisley, and green pants. A
pair of hoop earrings. Her clothes did not hang well and the
colors did not suit her. She felt large and awkward, loitering in
the big gym anyway, with this stranger who hardly opened his
mouth. It was obvious he was not impressed with her.
     Let's split, he said very soon.
Okay.
     Want to go to MacDonalds, have a coke?
No thanks. You can just take me home.
     Home?
He looked surprised.
Sure, she said, I have to sing in the choir tomorrow.

So he drove her home with the radio playing between them. She
found his indifference attractive. It implied a private life, and a
lack of concern for externals. She could slump.
     I don't come from around here either, she said.
Where from?
     Oh New Haven. At least it's a city.
I know what you mean.
     I'm not the country type.
I heard you were a little weird.
     That's right. That's me.

Around here, everyone's weird who comes from somewhere else, he said.

> Well, they didn't say you were weird. They said you were
> straight.

Whatever that means.

He pulled up in front of her house and turned off the engine. The radio continued playing. I like this song, he said and raised the volume. They listened in silence till it went off.

> I better go in, she said.

You ever want to make it? He stared at her through the darkness, but didn't lift a hand.

> Make it? You mean fuck?

I guess you could say that.

> You sure get right to the point.

Why beat around the bush?

> No reason. But no. Never, she said.

Okay.

He opened the car door and she walked behind him, smiling down, to her house. She lifted her head and laughed in his face before going inside.

Her mother was swaying tipsily against the hall wall, when Kathy came in.

> He looked like your Dad, she slurred, No good.

Kathy climbed the stairs laughing.

The next morning Kathy walked to the ten o'clock service at her church. She tested her singing voice, humming. It was nearly November. A bluejay sat on a mailbox. One lone figure was raking leaves down the way. The bluejay flew to the tip of an American flagpole and sat there, alert. The collection of ranch-style houses, which Randy helped build, was called Mainstream. Kathy, walking, was glad to leave them behind. Randy said he liked the 'serenity' of Ashville. Kathy said, 'serenity' was one word she reserved for graveyards.

The two words dwarf and divorce passed through her mind. When her Mom got a divorce, she married a dwarf. Rumpelstilskin. He stamped his foot when he got mad, which was often. Both words had a scary sound. Yawning, like a hole in the ground. No one should get a divorce, or marry a mean dwarf.

She quickened her stride, excited to be on her way to sing, and she thought of Father Steele, ahead, waiting for her to do her best. He had encouraged her from the start — to stand out solo with her voice. Her gift, he called it; and all gifts must be nurtured, as radios must be tuned.

He was a poor preacher, in fact, and not given to pompous sermons. More shy, stammered collages of quotes he liked — from Scripture and poetry and philosophy. People found his connections difficult to follow. He was suspected of being a Jew who converted.

"He has that look," Kathy heard people say.

He was dark of complexion and hair, of which he had a great deal, powerfully built. Stocky. In his late forties. He drew suspicious connections between the Old Testament and the New, insinuating that the Israelites were waiting for the Messiah then, much as the Gentiles are, now. He seemed to love Psalms as much as the Gospels. He was also a lover of music and literature and walked around the streets, reading 'in a rabbinical fashion'.

His face was square, its sallow color darkened by heavy creases and shades. Heavy eyebrows, a full sensual mouth without humor, but an expression of yearning, as if he had lost something terribly important. That's what Kathy thought. She was his constant defender. To her he stood out among the rich, cold and kempt people of Ashville as a reminder of history and suffering. And she felt, when he spoke to her, that he understood her in those terms.

His blond wife, everyone knew, was an atheist. She wouldn't go to church. Instead she sat with her small daughter, sipping sherry and developing photographs of leaves and flowers, which she took herself. The couple were, in a short span of time, considered a disaster for the tiny conservative parish.

"He's more in touch with reality than they are," Kathy muttered to herself, and to others, "Just because he doesn't go through all the fakey social bullshit you do, you hate him."

Once, after choir practice, he said to Kathy, "When you sing, it's as if God is singing through you. Wonderful!" Then he marched away, abruptly, as if he had just embarrassed the two of them. But Kathy was not embarrassed. Elated. The outer God she had formed for herself, was suddenly sucked inside, where it nested and fluttered and sang with her vocal chords. It was not that she was God, but that she had, inside, access to Its power.

Walking to church to sing was, then, an activity of great signifi cance to Kathy.

Kathy as usual entered the church by the side door and climbed the narrow wooden steps to the balcony where the choir sang. She was met by a screech of female voices, her friends from the choir.

"Did you hear what happened, did you hear?

Kathy backed against the organ, received the information that the Rector shot himself on Friday, and lied.

Sure. I knew already, she said and moved to her chair. She sat down and stared at the music.

The Service was conducted by a young minister from Bridgeport, who explained what had happened to those who did not know already. Havoc fluttered over the hymnal pages. Rigid postures briefly folded.

"The important thing to remember," said the young minister, "is that this event happened to him alone — not to you, not because of you. You must not, at all costs, confuse yourselves with his tragic act, but hold yourselves back, with generosity."

Then he announced that the service would proceed according to plan. And Kathy had to rise and sing:

The king of love my shepherd is
Whose goodness faileth never;
I nothing lack if I am his,
And he is mine forever.

The congregation followed, singing the other verses, and Kathy did not join in but stared at a stainglass image of John the Baptist dunking someone in water. She herself felt like a pane of glass.

But after the service she took her place beside the coffee-maker and focused on the new minister. His name was Lachlan St. George! He was the diametric opposite of Father Steele. Tall, relaxed, outdoorsy, with a ruddy face, small bright eyes and curling lips, he, at least made no pretense at mourning, like the others.

"Frankly," she heard him say, "I can't share your grief as I did not know the man."
Guilt-ridden parishoners swooped around, making plans for the Rector's family, only to discover the family had left already, the wife had collapsed and could not handle a funeral.
"We'll just do something simple then," they decided.
Well, I'm not going to any funeral, Kathy said to herself, and shuddered. She had the idea that suicide was catching, like an ordinary sickness, it slipped from mouth to mouth.
Sin spreads," Father Steele had said in a sermon.
She made a lunge for her coat, and was caught by the arm by the young minister.
Just a minute, he said, I wanted to make sure you'll be singing next week too. A lovely voice. Will you? I'll be here for awhile. I'd like that.
Sure, she said.
That's good, thank you, he said heartily.
She fled, feeling the church turn into a hospital for terminal patients, behind her.

She walked the long way home, repeating the minister's message about holding oneself back from the suicide. It seemed like a sensible thing to say, but it wouldn't penetrate, as truth, into the cold mausoleum she found inside herself. She looked at the details of the landscape around her — a forgotten apple freezing on one branch, roses blackening on a fence, a birdsong coming from a bird — and felt the Underworld pressing up against the lid of the Earth, a vault inside a shell, which she was walking over, a cracked surface, might be an empty egg. Hell was a fact of life right underfoot.

No rational questions entered her mind, regarding faith and suicide, despair and religion. The information had been received, the facts entered into her brain's ledger, indelible: Father Steele had put a bullet in his head on Friday. Some of her had, of course, been munched up by the ground around her, just as much as he knew of her, his information, about her, had gone; she was slightly less now than she had been. The fact that he did it deliberately, to himself, and it was not an accident, was, in its way insulting. No one was good enough for him, it seemed to say.

It was highway robbery too. He took off with himself. A form of theft, supernatural really. Then it bore some relation to a depraved sexual act, as if he had exposed himself, erect, from the pulpit.

She had no sympathy, he was now lower than a worm, but her fear of him stayed. He might be making an irresistable gesture in her direction. The sky, risible, was vast; the earth was round and eager. The wobbling plank, or so it seemed, she traversed, on her way home, could cave in, quickly, taking her whole self after, not just the little part the Reverend possessed, snatched and ran off with.

That fucking son of a bitch, she said.

Her Mom hunched over the oven, examining a roast, her long narrow back and slender shoulders, Kathy felt, unsuited to such menial labor.

Can I help? she asked her mother.

The oven door slammed, her Mom swung up to look at her, throwing back her dark brown, curled hair. Her face was rosy.

I guess you heard the news, she said.

Yup.

We found out yesterday, but didn't want to tell you.

Why not?

It might spoil you fun last night.

Ha, fun.

Well, you never know. Anyway, awful, wasn't it?

I mean, he must have been crazy.

No kidding.

But these things happen to religious people, too, you know, they go over the deep end. They're only human.

Her Mom explained every vile and weak act as being 'only human' as if her opinion of mankind was based only on the worst. She tended to ignore all struggles for change; they were aberrations against the desolate fate laid out for you. Kathy disapproved of this aspect of her Mom.

Go ahead and cry, said Mom.

What for.

Well, it's natural, to want to cry.

I'm sorry, I can't.

Later maybe, Mom smiled.

She pushed Kathy's hair back from her cheeks and examined her.

You always surprise me, honey.

I'll set the table.

She did so, her hands shaking.

So I turned and considered all the gross acts that are committed under the sun, and I shed tears, for all was vanity, and ego, and they could not be destroyed. I tried to sweep away the surface troubles, to cast away the stones and leaves that littered my pathway to Zion. I spat all the rash words off my tongue and tried to speak, only, of good, but then my mouth became as a spring shut up, and a fountain sealed. I looked into my garden where spikenard, saffron, camphire, calamus and cinnamon should bloom, and saw my garden shrivelled and messy. Where was the well of living waters? Where were the streams from Lebanon? I was an American, I put on my coat, I washed my feet and went into the garden. I would work there till all the ancient spices should return, but they didn't. I was like one cursed. The roof of my mouth, like the garden, dried up, and failed me. I was repeating my faults daily. I tried to rid myself of ego and vanity, but unlike the fishpools in Heshbon, I was full of shit. The joints of my thighs were like rusty gates. My body, like a broken wall, let the enemy climb in and over. There was no protection. What I saw to be evil, on the outside, grew up in me, on the inside. I looked to the left and I looked to the right, but I could not look straight up, for the sky, undefiled like the breast of a dove, rejected me. He that observeth the wind shall not sow; and she that regardeth the clouds shall not reap. Those that see the purity of outer space shall long for nothing less. But the tree falls to the north, and the tree falls to the south, and wherever it falls, it stays, locked to the earth and spreading corruption. Whoever tries to lift the tree and remove it, a serpent will bite him. So there is no way but by stealth and delusion, and if my body falls where no one lifts it, dead flies will cause the folly of my flesh to send forth a stinking odor. Gross! Some will call it Wonderful, for it will smell like their flesh too.

✛

Kathy considered calling Elmer. Back. For three days she hovered around the telephone. The idea was that he was a blank slate. She knew all the other boys in town. But Elmer was a fresh start, and she had this sudden craving for love. To have her heart's tremors restored to a healthy thump and to be stroked and praised, audibly. That would be love. To neck ad nauseum and then go all the way.

Sure, let's make it, let's fuck, she might say. Why not? Her faith had been struck a blow. She couldn't get over this suicide thing, a mortal blow. It ate her inside out. But it was the thought of love as an antidote that got her through the first three days. The thought turned out to be sufficient. She had trained herself, already, to say No at the last minute to the pleas of boys. Now she could say No to her own pleas, in silence, at home.

The struggle disconnected her. After school she wandered the streets, along the edge of the green, her posture hunched, her face pinched. On the fourth day she passed the new minister, Lachlan St. George, coming out of a sporting goods store. Though she raised her hand in greeting, he didn't catch the gesture or register recognition. He walked by, tall and glowing, and she withered, watching him depart.

She slipped into a gift shop, followed by her fat friend, Frieda, and shoplifted for the first time. A pair of silver moon earrings.
  I don't like stealing from the small local shops, Frieda said.
  I usually go out to the mall with Sally, Beth and Joanne.
  Next time try it out there.
Okay, that's a good idea, said Kathy. But she felt no guilt. She felt insolent instead. To be outside the law of man was to enter the law of God. That is, getting something for nothing was like a miracle — unnatural, illegal, blissful. She knew she would do it again.

✝

On Wednesday afternoon, she went to the church at the usual time for choir practice. But there was a hearse full of flowers outside and rows of shiney cars lining the streets. Father Steele's funeral.

I wouldn't be caught dead at a funeral, she said.

Not his, mine, or anyone else's.

And she walked all the way to the mall on the highway, though the air was cutting and cold. Steele, steal.

On Thursday, she went to the church again, and this time she met the minister inside. He was putting out on a table the mimeo'd notices of Sunday's service. She came up behind him awkwardly.

Excuse me.

He turned and took a second to recognize her, this time he did. Smiling he said hello.

I wondered, just, when choir practice is.

We're going to put it off till next week, he told her pleasantly, I'm glad you asked. It's in this notice here. With all this confusion, we can't really practice this week.

Next Wednesday?

Yes, at the usual time. Okay?

Yeah, fine.

I'm glad you asked, he said again.

She could see, up close, he was as flawed as most people, but, still, there was a warmth to his person which blurred the effects of creases and bumps.

Shrugging self-consciously, she turned and walked out. A sadness had risen in her looking at him. Not to be explained. Her mother would call it 'adolescent moodiness', how so often she was engulfed by emotion. She walked, aimlessly, around town and out along the highway, and by chance she passed the filling station where Elmer worked. She recognized him through her eyes stinging, but turned her face askance quickly, praying he wouldn't see her. Oh love, where is thy sting? She had, at home, awaiting her, bean bag chairs, the stamping Randy, an intoxicated mother and two wicked stepbrothers who stared at t.v. and stuffed their faces after school. She wondered if this nauseating vision was the one that compelled Father Steele to blow himself away.

What you need is a good fuck, her friend Sally would say. That word, fuck, permeated every piece of dialogue she engaged in, she used it as much as anyone else. But what did it really signify? I want love. She thought. The darkening sky came down. Nobody loves me. She hurried home.

Shoplifting was a fairly common occurence, among girls Kathy's age. They did it without any sense of criminality or immorality; they just didn't want to get caught. They covered for each other, keeping a look-out, and devised dressing-room thefts over lunch at school. In their eyes the marketplace was the epitome of corruption. If called upon to justify their stealing, they would reply, "the prices are a rip-off" and "no one cares about this crap anyway." This crap was by and large the clothing and jewelry found at the large shopping mall on the highway. Salespeople were non-existent. Rack upon rack, counter upon counter of mass-produced material stretched out before them. Sometimes the girls would go to the shoe section and exchange the pair they wore in for a new pair to wear out. Why not? "The new pair will fall apart, like the old one, in a couple of weeks anyway. It's all crap!" And they marched out, heads high, not stopping to laugh till they were hidden by a sea of cars. Kathy's digression into shoplifting, therefore, was not a complete aberration. Although she thought it was.

The boys Kathy usually dated were ones she had known since her arrival in Ashville. They were her age, and had to be her height or taller. One was so conceited, he had few friends; the other was a former jock with a back injury; and the third was a thin intellectual who had applied to Ivy League colleges. All of them had the same relationship with Kathy. That is, they found her reassuringly boyish, easy to be silent with, and surprisingly passionate in spite of the word 'stop'.

None of them had gotten as far as a hand on a bare breast. But she kissed long and well, and was warm and affectionate. They all stopped dating her without any hard feelings, but because, in some mysterious sense, the relationship was perfect and required no more attention. Still they would stand with a hand on her shoulder, at the edge of a field, and be comfortable there.

Kathy, for her part, missed affection when it vanished. She liked being stroked and fondled by a friend; she had no drive to experience 'the big O', not yet, it seemed like too much work. But there was real pleasure in necking, and sometimes she eyed a familiar boy's face with a touch of yearning. What would it be like with him, she wondered, waiting, incapable of flirtation.

This stealing phenomenon gave her a stranger feeling than lust did. It was her first experience with calculated evil, and made her supremely conscious of the gap between emotion and reason. Since she could talk herself, alongside her friends, into justifying any action, she figured she was capable of doing any number of wrongs. That was not a pleasant feeling. Far better to imagine herself compelled.

In psychology class she had learned that the unconscious controls behavior. That seemed like a luxurious method of reasoning to Kathy now. She was only too aware that she could stop herself from stealing any more. She was equally aware that she could not stop herself from thinking about Father Steele. Her memory was out of control, but not the effect of her present thought on her future action. Yet the more she thought of not-stealing, the more interesting self-disobedience became. That, of course, was called compulsion.

What would happen, then, she wondered, if she were offered a tilt in the hay with some guy like Elmer? What if he tried it again? She was scared she would find herself sliding along and then feeling unbearable remorse.

I need a moral adviser, she kept telling herself, urgently.

Lachlan St. George telephoned his mother in Boston and said, "I hope I survive life in exurbia."

"Don't worry, Darling, you will," she said.

"I am rather interested in the problems of teenagers living out here," he said.

"Yes, why don't you make a study of it?"

"I don't know about 'a study'. But I do think I can learn something. God knows what."

He stared out the window at the leafy, lonely Green and sighed for the city life he had left behind.

Kathy, too, often sighed for the city life she left behind. New Haven was not the hottest little city in the States, but it contained Yale, pockets of green dignity, to which you could aspire, as a townie. Also, there were movies, restaurants and interesting stores. A train, too, to New York City which you could hear, from the apartment where they lived then, passing by the hour. She had been dragged to Ashville against her will and often cursed her real father, inwardly, for forcing this new life on herself and her mother.

Vacuuming, she told her mother, I can't stand it here.
Well you'll be graduating soon, said Mom.
But if I go away, I'll miss you!
I have to stay with Randy now, Honey, I owe him alot.
Like your life, Kathy muttered.

She longed to leave, but dreaded the break with her mother. Just a matter of months, and she didn't have a plan in the world. The others did; but she expected her future would be revealed to her by divine intervention, and waited impatiently for that day.
"Life is unfair," wrote John F. Kennedy.
No kidding, Kathy remarked.

TWO

*

What Elmer saw, everywhere, was speed and cruelty. His eyes held the expression of a small boy in an overcrowded day care. Help!? He would have been an artisan in any year. Automechanics suited him. Weights, results, tools that fit onto other tools, grease, no small talk. He had little to say to anyone about anything, except cars. His boss, Sam, did all the talking at the service station and knew everyone in town. Elmer stayed crammed under hoods or under the whole body of the car like a miner with a beam. A radio played music close to his ear.

Sam was heavy-set and grey, red in the face from good air and whiskey. An even-tempered man is pleasant to work for; and he seemed to respect Elmer's privacy. But one day he told Elmer,
        "I want you to do the road work for awhile."
He gave Elmer the keys to the pick-up and the calls as they came in. Flat tires, dead batteries.
        "This is just temporary," he assured Elmer.
Sam was breaking in a new boy on the pumps.
        "I don't like it," said Elmer
but did as he was told. Being sent out to cope with some human trouble meant contact, which he didn't enjoy. But it also meant some more money from the affable Sam, and money was hope.

*

Monday morning, at eight o'clock, Elmer had to go to the house of a young woman — set way back in the woods. Her car wouldn't start, a Chevy only three years old, it was either the generator or the battery. She had to get her kid to school. Elmer charged her battery off the truck, she gave him five bucks and he went back to the station. The next morning, she called again. Same problem. He bumped on out down the dirt road. The leaves were turning red.It was chilly.

"Must be you need a new battery," he told her.

"How much will it cost?

"About thirty-five."

She sighed a banner of frosty air. He glanced at her with mild sympathy, figuring she lived alone with her child. She had that baleful look.

"Bring her down to the station," he said, "and I'll give her a long charge. See if that works. If it doesn't, we'll have to put in a new one."

She agreed, he got her car started and she followed him back into town, her son at her side. She left the car at the station with Elmer and walked on to the boy's school. He was pretty sure she was going to need a new battery, but didn't say so. She came back to the office in a half hour, Elmer was gone, so Sam sent her off in the car which seemed to be running fine now.

*

The third morning she called again.

"I guess I'll need a new battery," she said to Elmer.

"I guess so. I'll be right out," he said.

The day was grey, eminently wintery, although leaves clung to most branches. He noticed a few pleasing features about the landscape, a stone wall, a thin river with a duck family scattered on the bank, tufty green grass silvered by dew and somebody's vegetable garden with a few bright tomatoes and drooping sunflowers on the stalks. Down the road beyond the river then he saw the woman waiting with her son, by the Chevy. She had blue-black hair, straight like the Japanese, an olive complexion, she wore a Navy blue pea-jacket and jeans, sneakers. She smiled, her boy jumped up and down.

"Sorry," said Elmer.

"It's not your fault."

"Well, kind of."

She had already raised the hood of her car, he hooked up the cable to his truck. She got in and started her engine, he got out of the truck, unhooked it, slammed down the hood and went to her car window.

"Follow me in," he said.

She followed him down the road, he eyed her through the rear-view window. He wondered how she made a living. How she ended up out here. He came from the Southwest, realized she might be Chicano, she didn't look like she belonged in a town like this one, unfriendly to strangers unless they looked like the offsprings of Vikings.

"I won't charge you for the road work," he told her at the station.

"Thanks alot."

Now what are you going to do — with your boy, I mean."

"Take him on to school."

"How will you get home?"

"I can walk."

"No wait," he said, "This won't take long. You can just come back and wait here."

She picked up her son, who was half her size, and set off down the road to school. Just then Elmer got another road call and, cursing, went off in the truck.

When he got back she was sitting in the office, smoking and reading a paperback. She smiled at him, with reserve, and he got to work on her car. He was asking her imaginary questions while he worked, but knew he wouldn't ask her any of them aloud. He had a couple of buddies, casual, in the town, who sometimes arranged a date for him with some High School girl. He only went along with it to show he was normal. But he was bored by young girls and scared of women; women he felt were smarter than he was and could put him down, in a flash, one crack. This one looked intelligent, independent, her book, her house, her child. But then there was that baleful side, in her eyes, she was too small to live alone.

"On the other hand, she might be married," he said to himself.

*

Elmer rented two furnished rooms over an antique shop on the main highway. He brought his clothes to the cleaners. He saved most of his money. He was very interested in money. He worked long hours and would happily work longer. He put his money in savings, what he didn't need to live on, and checked on its growth frequently. Since he had come to Asheville, six months before, he had amassed several thousand dollars. It was only a matter of careful budgeting and temperate living, both of which came naturally to him.

The other guys around town, whom he knew casually, lived at home still. They talked alot about money; some of them worked; but they blew all their earnings and slept off the effects of hard drinking nights in their childhood beds. Elmer thought they were the dregs. They had mixed feelings about him. He was so independent, he was exclusive; there was no access to the center of his character. He came from the West; they knew that much, and they were suspicious of his being in Ashville at all. He had acquired one of the better jobs, but he was an outsider. Sometimes they would set him up with a High School girl, for a date, but he never went further than that. He was always talking about "splitting" — heading South, when the weather got too cold.

When the garage closed at eight, he usually went home with a pizza and pored over maps. He had a collection of maps that took up a two-by-four carton. He would tack one up on his wall and, listening to the radio or the television behind him, he would trail his finger along back roads and highways all the way into Mexico.

"I've been on the road since I was thirteen. Not about to stop now," he would say.

*

Another thing Elmer thought alot about was D – TH. The very word gave him problems sleeping. His maps used to put him to sleep, like a tranquilizer, or a book, but they didn't anymore. Since he came to Ashville, he was troubled by insomnia. He would lie awake thinking about D – TH. He had seen two D – D bodies in his life. One had choked, a member of his family, the other was just plain D – D. Until he came to Ashville, he didn't think much about either case, but something in this Northern climate brought out the morbid in him. He looked at maps of the North, all the way beyond the province of Quebec, and literally shivered, thinking of that landscape approaching ice. Ice and sleep were allied. Both were half-way zones between being and nothingness. He didn't like this. He had a bad feeling that D – TH was just another version of LIFE. There would never be complete escape to freedom. He felt, alone in his bed, like a disassembled machine. Only the sun could slip his joints together and get him moving again. Then he would keep his nose to the grindstone, at work, all day, and concentrate on other machines.

When he heard about Father Steele's suicide, Elmer was confirmed in his attitudes on Protestant preachers. He had given the man gas, fixed his engine, and had suspected him of fraud on sight.
    "He's just pretending he believes in God," Elmer said to himself, and to Sam, "It's all show. The collar. The black suit. He wants to look good to hide how bad he is."
The suicide was the proof of that particular pudding. Everyone was talking about it.

    "Don't be too hard on him," Sam told Elmer, "He was given a pretty hard time by his congregation. Myself I go to St. Mary's and don't know much about Episcopalians. But I do know the people around here were out to get him."

Elmer's eyes widened. He didn't like premature judgement

IN THE MIDDLE OF NOWHERE

when he heard it from the mouths of others, and even less when he heard it from himself.

"Still," he muttered defensively, "I think suicide is bad. It's like a black hole in space, or something. It pulls everything around it inside."

"True enough," said Sam.

Elmer continued to mull on the question for some time. He wanted to really know what he himself thought about it, since D—TH was so much on his mind these days. But all he came up with was more of the same: harsh judgement, revulsion.

"Maybe he was d—d already," he concluded.

The wintery sky made him shudder. He tried to envision tropical landscapes, great flowers pitted in spears of palm. Snow was so strange, unnecessary to nature as he knew it. Covering the names of roads and plants, as well as the roads and plants themselves, snow.

"It never snows," said Sam, "till after Thanksgiving."

Elmer immediately chalked up Thanksgiving as a good time for his departure from Ashville. Going south, following the heat, was the one constant plan he had in his life. It was routine. He had come east to Ashville in spring. Just to see what the east was like, on his way to the south Atlantic coast, where he was sure he belonged. Florida. The Keys. Louisiana. The Gulf. Those names called him on, the way Money, A New Life, A Break call on others. He had some reason for this.

His mother came from New Orleans. She called him Sunny in a drawl, making sure he understood what the word signified, when he was small. A tow-headed boy. Alone with his dark-haired mother and her brother in Wyoming. After she died, he wrote her letters which his uncle mailed. He had been garrulous, but then he turned quiet, writing the letters till he grew tired of getting no answer, and stopped. His eyes startled—permanently—by the revealing silence.

*

One Saturday afternoon Elmer went to Penny Saver to buy himself some socks. A warehouse department store, articles for sale lay in heaps, seemingly abandoned, no one was ever around to help. Elmer passed through the lingerie section on his way to Men's Clothes and saw that girl Kathy dropping panties into her purse. He was embarrassed; he could see she was shoplifting, brazenly; and he didn't want her to see him. He grabbed his socks and paid for them. When he went out into the cold parking area, there was Kathy, on the sidewalk, a small man in gray was looking at the contents of her bag. She had been caught! Elmer hurried, head down, to his car. Once inside, he could see Kathy being led back into Penny Saver by the little man whose hands were full of panties.

*

Saturday afternoons Elmer worked at the station. He was out by the pumps when the woman with the Chevy drove in.

Hi there, she said cheerfully.

She wanted some gas and an oil check.

Where's your boy today, asked Elmer.

With his Dad, she said.

Elmer nodded and raised the hood. She got out of the car and came over to look inside with him.

The battery okay? he asked.

Oh, fine, but now something else is wrong.

What.

It keeps backfiring, chugging.

Might be the spark plugs.

It needs a tune-up.

We've got a special on tune-ups.

When should I bring it in?

Monday morning.

She agreed and got back into the car. He slammed down the hood and started cleaning her windshield. Their eyes met, he looked away from the glass, embarrassed. He remembered her name on her check; it was Caralisa; there was no man's name over it. When she handed him the money, he cleared his throat.

You from the Southwest? he asked.

Tucson, she said.

Your name, you know, I thought.

I know, it is.

Right.

You from out there too?

Sort of, he said. See you Monday.

Take care, she smiled.

*

Sunday Elmer came down with the flu. Chills, fever, cramps, he just lay in bed and watched movies on television. Slept, nightmares, woke up, slept again. At first he wondered if he had lost his mind and was not really sick at all; maybe this was the way he always felt, but just hadn't admitted it to himself. He certainly couldn't remember feeling well. On the other hand, he hardly ever got sick. It scared him, being sick, alone, as if he were old and disposable. So on Monday morning he got up anyway, dizzy, and set off for work. He hadn't eaten for twenty four hours.

You look awful, said Sam, Go home.

I'm okay.

I don't want to catch it, whatever it is.

Elmer got in his car just as the woman Caralisa in the Chevy pulled into the station. He leaped out to meet her.

Listen, I'm not feeling too hot.

I guess not, she said eyeing his face.

You can leave it in anyway.

No, I'll wait. I want you to do it.

Bring it in on, uh, Wednesday?

Sure. Hey, take care!

She really looked concerned, he noted.

He carried her concern home with him. But he felt like a tractor had run over his body, aching, even with aspirin, in bed all day. Soon he couldn't remember anyone who cared for him, but wanted his mother to come back to life and take care of him. It was maddening that she couldn't do that much, just one small trick, for his sake now, and enter the room with a cold towel. If she would, he would forgive her for dying in the first place. The sun began to drop, fast, faster than it should. He watched it go, fearfully, and flipped on *Star Trek* to replace it.

The dark room was dark with words and images. The word 'succor' that meant help, that they used about Jesus, 'succor', and 'sucker' that he used about himself, and 'suck' that was written on the wall in the men's room at the service station, 'suck', and 'succotash' which he hated. He lurched into an upright position and focused his eyes on the television screen. He thought he had seen the woman with the Chevy there, for a flash, looking back at him.

Tuesday morning Elmer was better, but not all right. He went out and got himself some tea and donuts from Donut City; he also bought the town weekly to look at ads for automobiles. In the Police Blotter, they noted a girl had been picked up for shoplifting at Penny Saver, but they didn't give her name.

Elmer looked at a map of the Yucatan for a time, then dozed, and dreamed about Caralisa. The dream was all feeling, and little action, onslaughts of pleasure rushing to his fever. The setting was like an Arizona fortified with red triangular pyramids and although there was nothing sexual about the dream, when he woke up, he was mortified by its contents. He was actually afraid Caralisa might see through him, into the dream, as through a glass window, the next day.

*

Wednesday was clear blue and cold, the sky like a glass of water. Elmer had recovered from the flu and got to the station early with his coffee and donuts. Sam's wife – Lily – was there instead of Sam.

"Sam's got the flu," she said.

She said she was going to work on the books, and she'd help out on the pumps, if necessary. Lily was a plump woman with bleach blond hair, cheerful. Her presence transformed the atmosphere around the station, making Elmer feel awkward. She liked to talk alot, and luckily the new boy attendant didn't seem to mind, but lounged against the door, listening to her.

When the Chevy pulled in, Elmer waved the car into the service area. Caralisa climbed out, pulling her son after her, and Elmer followed them into the office. Lily said *Hi, Dear* to Caralisa.

"And what's your name?" she asked the little boy.

"David," he said.

"Cute! Does he go to school?"

"Kindergarten," said Caralisa.

"You live near town?"

"Out near the orchards."

"That's a pretty area. Been around long?"

"O just since July."

"Never saw you before," said Sam's wife. "Does your husband work in town?"

Elmer now stood by the door, listening.

"No, but I teach, one day a week."

"Oh! Where?"

Caralisa glanced back at Elmer as if for help.

"At the State Pen," she said.

We better get to work on your car, said Elmer.

How long will it take?

Most of the morning.

I'll come back around noon then, she said.

Elmer stepped out of the office with her; she picked up her son.
    Isn't he kind of heavy?
But warm, too, she smiled.
    You going to walk all the way home?
I'll leave him at school first.
    Doesn't your husband have a car?
I'm not married, she said.
And goodbye, as he walked back to work on her car, thinking he should tell her, some time, not to give strangers information like that. There was, for him, something familiar about her. An expression, a posture — he wasn't sure which, or if it was her situation. She suggested a kind of childishness, in spite of her age, which he was drawn to. She seemed to treat her son more like a brother than a child of her own. A lost quality, too, to both of them.

*

Just after eleven, the Chevy was ready for Caralisa. Elmer was
writing up the bill, when Lily said,
"Hey, there's the new minister."
Elmer looked out the window and saw the dull green Buick
driven by Lachlan St. George cruise in and stop beside the
pumps.
"He's just temporary, but they might try to keep him on
    too. He's a good-looker," she whispered.
"I'll take care of him," said Elmer.

Lachlan St. George was not wearing a collar, but a checkered
flannel lumberjacket, longish brown hair. Like a student in animal husbandry, not a minister. He stood up outside his car and
smiled rosily at Elmer.
"Fill her up with unleaded please," he said.
He moved, tall, to the pump with Elmer.
"You get all the town business here?"
"Just about," said Elmer.
"Beautiful day."
Elmer stared at the flickering numbers on the pump. Out of the
corner of hie eye, he saw Caralisa coming, in navy blue, across
the road and his throat jumped. Then he noted the minister
watching her, rocking on his heels, he was wearing big, lacy,
leather, expensive boots. Elmer put the cap back on the tank.
The Minister gave him a twenty and Elmer walked into the
office for change, without acknowledging Caralisa. He ran up
the register and through the plate glass window saw the minister
chatting with her. Elmer took a quick dislike to him, he didn't
like religious men anyway, they were hypocrites in their collars.
This one was a hypocrite without a collar, acting too chummy,
eager to prove himself a regular guy. Elmer brought him his
change with a sullen look.

"I'll be seeing you again, I'm sure," said the young minister
    to Elmer, "I've just moved into town."
"Yeah?" Dully.

"I'm pretty new here too," said Caralisa.

"That makes three of us," Elmer said to the ground.

"Be seeing you then," the minister put in, this time to Caralisa.

But he got in his car and drove off, leaving Elmer alone, at last, with her.

Is my car ready? she asked.

She should be fine now.

For awhile.

Yeah, even the new ones make trouble.

She trailed him into the office where he rooted around for the invoice.

You really work hard, she said, don't you.

I guess so.

You don't look all well yet.

It was just the flu, nothing much.

What was it like?

Aching bones mostly.

Help, I think I'm getting it.

He glanced at her quickly: It's all over town, he said.

I have to go to work.

If you have it, you can't.

He handed her the slip and she went into her purse for her checkbook. Her black hair fell across her cheeks, hiding her eyes; Elmer took a good look.

Do you like to teach? he asked.

No, but I get a little money.

From the State Pen?

Well, they're not dogs, you know, they don't just turn into dogs, as soon as they're locked up.

Sure, I know that.

I don't feel too hot, was how she explained her anger.

You live all alone?

Well, with David.

You should be careful, he said.

Getting sick just happens.

No, I mean.

About people?

Well, yeah.

I know.

I mean, even in the country.

Oh well.

That was a minister, he said.

Didn't seem like one.

That's what I mean.

She hunched over the cash register, writing out her check, and Elmer leaned against the doorjam, his knees shakey.

What do you teach?

American history.

Where's the prison?

Facility near Providence.

Long way to go.

One day a week, it's money. All the extra I'm allowed to make, you know, on Welfare.

She tossed back her hair, handing the check over, and flashed a smile which turned into a grimace.

I feel awful, she said.

Look kind of pale.

I better —

Go on home.

From the hook on the wall, he got down her car keys and walked outside with her.

Listen, he said.

What.

If you need something.

Well, I might, if I'm sick.

Just call.

He walked away, breathing hard over his courage.

*

She called him the next morning, early, the same time she called when her car was breaking down.

I'm sorry, she said, Can you take my son to school?

Sure, okay.

He told Lily he had a road call and left in the pick-up. When he got there, he noticed her house was more of a shack than anything else really. Grey clapboard. The boy was waiting at the door with his coat on.

Where's your mother? asked Elmer.

In there.

Come on in! she called.

She was sitting on a couch wrapped up in a blanket watching the morning news on television. There were lights on, as the place was essentially gloomy, surrounded by trees. It smelled of cigarette smoke and firewood, all damp.

You should turn on the heat, he said.

I didn't order oil yet.

It's cold.

I know.

Need anything?

Just time to rest.

What time do I bring him home?

He's done at eleven thirty.

I'll give him lunch at the station.

Hey, thanks.

Okay.

The little boy was all excited by riding in the truck. He wiggled around, but didn't ask questions. He didn't look like his mother, except for the shape of his face and maybe his finely pursed mouth. His hair was straight and brown like the cap on an acorn. Elmer never had a father himself and carried no concepts as to the kind of talk that went on between a man and a boy. No talk was fine with him. He just told him to sit still, let him out of the truck in front of the school and told him he'd be back to get him. He watched the boy walk, turning in circles, round and round, up to the front of the building, and felt sorry for him.

*

It took two days for Caralisa to recover. Elmer brought the boy to school both days and then back to the station for lunch, where he was no trouble. He didn't smile alot, but followed Elmer around gracefully, quietly, watching all that he did.
    "That little guy thinks you're God," said Lily.
    "Where's his father?"
    "They're divorced, I guess."
    "Oohh."
She smiled fully, insinuating romance was in the air.
    "His mother looks foreign. Is she?"
    "No, she's American," said Elmer.
    "Alot of Americans look foreign, I guess."

On Saturday afternoon, Caralisa called the station and Elmer answered the phone.
    "Is that you?" she asked.
"It's me," he said.
    "Can you come for supper tonight?"
"I guess so," he said.
    "I've got to repay you somehow, now that I'm better."
"No, you don't."
    "Well, come anyway."
When he hung up, Elmer wondered, suspiciously at once, why she assumed he was free on a Saturday night. When he got what he wanted, he was always suspicious. She might want to ask him to fix her car again, this time for nothing, or take care of David again. She didn't act flirtatious, but casual, as if they were the same sex. It must be their age difference, he decided, that made her take him for granted. He was just twenty, but she looked close to thirty in the sun. He figured she thought he was just a kid, even if he could do things she couldn't do, and she was just being sisterly, nice. He tried to avoid imagining she might like him, want him, need him: it was a system he had constructed a long time ago, a way of avoiding the worst emotion possible — one that had no name.

*

Her shack looked lonely in the night. A few little lights in the windows, all around black trees, a clear sky full of stars. There was only a thick smell of apples in the air. She let him in at once. David was still awake, but tucked in his bed in a tiny side room. Elmer stepped over some toys and told him to go to sleep. The shack inside smelled of cooking.

I'm a vegetarian, she told him, I hope you won't mind.

I eat anything.

Wine?

No, I don't drink, thanks.

She gave him some grape soda and drank wine herself, and smoked while she cooked. The radio was tuned to a rock station from New York. There was one round table, where he sat down.

You look better, he said.

So do you.

He began, nervously, talking about money, his money, how much he made; then he asked her about her financial situation. Economics, for Elmer, was the key to human behavior. How a person made a living, what they did with what they earned, how much they wanted to make — these were the measurements of character. Caralisa told him she was on Welfare, but supplemented her check with this job in the prison; facts he already knew about her. She said she was used to being poor, didn't mind as long as she could get by. There was something, to Elmer, incomplete about this account.

I never knew nobody who was used to being poor, he said, unless they were secretly wealthy.

Well, my old man gives me a hand-out here or there, but mainly he just pays the Welfare Department, and then they pay me.

So that's how it works.

Well, till David's six. Then I have to get a job.

Why doesn't your husband support you instead of the Government? Or wasn't he your husband?

Sure. We were married. He just wanted to do it this way, and it's all the same to me. We can't deal with each other directly.

David will be six next year, right?

Right.

Well, then what?

She looked a little offended, hands on her hips. She was wearing white corduroy pants and an Italian knit jersey with orange stripes, a boyish body, but stylish. Nothing she did to herself could be haphazard, he guessed.

I don't know, she said.

Do you have some special interest, a hobby?

No! — breaking into laughter.

So what'll you do?

First I've got to make a really important decision.

What's that?

She pulled a pie out of the oven, then a casserole made of brown rice and black beans. In the fridge, she had a big salad made. Elmer made no move to help, she seemed so jittery and eager to be doing something with her hands.

What's your sign? she asked, head up.

He didn't understand.

You know. What month were you born?

Oh, I guess I'm Aries, they say.

Well, I'm Libran and Librans can't make decisions. They juggle all the issues until it's too late and circumstances have made the decision for them. So they tend to go around in a state of regret, or anger. It's frustrating.

She put plates in front of him.

So what's the decision you can't make? he asked.

It's unbelievable.

Go on.

Well, its about David. Is he asleep?

She went and peered into the boy's bedroom and came back with some satisfaction. She sat down beside Elmer with her wine and her food. It didn't look too good to him, but he began to eat self-consciously, hand on his knee.

His father, she said, has offered to take him. At least, he's putting alot of pressure on me, now that he's settling down with a wife.

Elmer kept on eating. It was spicey, not bad.

Part of me says no, and the other part says yes. Don't be shocked. I mean, it might be good for David, no matter how upset I would be, or how guilty I would feel. I don't know, I just can't decide, and in the meantime, Bob is looking for a lawyer, so I probably won't have a chance to make up my mind.

Elmer looked at her quickly.

Why are you living out here, he asked.

To get away from Bob, the pressures — just to work things out, you know.

Now she began to eat, and Elmer couldn't think of a thing to say. He could hardly swallow. What she had said to him was not shocking, but all too familiar. Women, girls, he had known, if only briefly, always carried some problem around like this, but usually much worse. Deserted, beaten, pregnant, poor, without families, no jobs, no citizenship, a drug or drinking problem, abortion, attempted suicide, an unwanted child, it was all he ever encountered in women. How could he be shocked by this relatively mild problem?

Do what you want, he finally said.

I don't know what I want.

She threw some salad onto his plate and some on hers, gulped her wine, attacked her food hungrily. He went into a daze, gazing at the greens on his plate, temporarily suspended, as it happened to him sometimes, especially eating, in a diner, some fast food spot, he would fade out listening to the voices of those around him. The stories he had heard!

It's a tough one, isn't it, she said.

Really, he agreed.

Oh well.

Something.

Will happen.

I mean, it always does, said Elmer.

She stretched back in her chair, smiling at him, and he felt, at once, she might disappoint him somehow. He had travelled enough to know that the stories told by those you meet on the road are not a fair representation of the whole character, but just a morsel. Sometimes the same morsel would be offered up

again and again, because there was nothing else there, and
sometimes people came along with magnificent stories about
themselves, their achievements, setbacks and mysteries, which
would hold you enthralled. But those people were often emptier
even than the ones who offered one solid morsel. In either case,
it would be a bore, and a destroying ordeal, being with anyone
of them all of the time. Since he didn't talk much, he heard alot.
But he didn't feel he knew much more now, about identifying
fraud, than he did when he first set out at thirteen. To know it,
you had to be its victim, and by then you wished you never had
to find out in the first place.

She put an apple pie on the table in front of the television and
beckoned him over to join her. They ate the pie there, side by
side, watching The Saturday Night Movie of the Week. When it
was over, he said he had better be on his way.
     And you be careful, he added.
What for? I am.
     Living out here alone.
I feel safe.
     That's a dangerous feeling.
Okay, she laughed, but listen.
     What.
Who was that minister I was talking to that day?
     I don't know. He just took over for some other priest who
     blew his brains out. Why?
Who blew his brains out?
     Some priest, I don't know, crazy.
Jesus.
     So what about this one?
I just thought he might be able to advise me on my problem —
you know, about David.
Elmer stood up, a slight flare in his eyes.
     Shit. He doesn't know anything.
He might. Sometimes they do.
     That's when they shoot themselves, he said.
He walked to her door quickly, and she followed, smaller by far,
a look of alarm on her face.

Keep in touch, she said.

Sure.

I'll tell you what I decide.

Do that.

Oh. By the way, she murmured. What's your name?

THREE

"When did you begin stealing?"

"About two weeks ago."

"Do you have any idea why?"

"Not really except that I like to."

"Like to, how?"

"A build-up, excitement, you know."

"Do you get an allowance?"

"Fifteen dollars a month."

"And that isn't enough?"

"I suppose so."

"You must realize how dangerous it is to steal."

"I do!"

"Are you going to go on doing it?"

"No, never."

"Okay. Then it won't go any further than these four walls."
He glanced at the white walls, then at the girl's face. It was
mobile even in repose. Bright eyes, a quiver inside her lips. Just
the barest hint of rebellion, the rest of her appearance was
ordinary. He was curious.

"What about your family? Do they ever come to Church,
to hear you sing, say?"

"No."

"Your father. What does he do?"

"My stepfather. Runs a construction company."

"Sisters? Brothers?"

"Two stepbrothers."

"When did your mother remarry?"

"About — ah — two years ago."

"Do you like your stepfather, family?"

"Well —"

"No?"

"No, Father."

She flashed a smile at him, then went serious. He was pleased
she would not cry.

"Listen, Kathy — you can call me Lachlan, not Father — I
hope you'll come down here more often, help me out, say.

I'm very interested in adolescents — they're my thing, so to speak. I want to start a teenager's talk session one evening a week, in the parish house. You could be a help to me."

She wasn't looking at him, but at her hands. The greyish pallor of her face, traces of terror, slowly ebbed into rosiness before his eyes. A small smile crossed her lips.

"I notice there's no place to hang out here, at night, nothing really to do. I know the rec center has various organized events, but I gather no one really goes there. Why not?"

"Oh it's stupid," she said, "They have things like cooking and macrame and a big pool table where the guys are supposed to hang out. But its all supervised, you know, *stupid*."

"What do you think would be a good kind of thing for people your age?"

"Somewhere just to, you know, sit around. Without someone staring at us. Like you say, a kind of casual place."

"I see," he said and then, "How old are you?"

"Seventeen."

"What will you do when you graduate?"

"I don't know."

"No college plans?"

"Well, my grades are blah, and I don't have any special interest yet. You know, no big ambition."

"I understand," he said.

Then he stood up, tall, and enjoined her to return on Wednesday night, at seven, to help him plan the teenage rap session. He asked her to bring along some friends. Kathy, rising, finally looked at him.

"Thank you," she said.

"I hope I've been of some help," he said, "And please tell your mother I'll call to assure her that you won't repeat the offense."

"Yes, Father."

"Lachlan."

"Lachlan."

She moved to the door, hesitently, gazing up at him.

"Uh, ah, can you, uh, tell me something, please."

"I'll try. What is it?"

"Why did Father Steele do that?"

"I can't tell you why, Kathy, but I hear he was a lonely sort of man."

"But I mean was he trying to get closer to God, or was he, you know, fallen from Grace?"

"A good question. But I think most suicides are committed without rhyme or reason, or despair, and the best thing you can do is pray for him."

"I guess so," she said. "I thought he knew everything, though."

"Well, I hope, for our sakes, he didn't," smiling.

Kathy didn't smile back, but registered some shock at this remark. It gave her grief, which she couldn't explain, so she put it away.

When she was gone, Lachlan roamed in circles around the small office. A crucifix hung on the wall behind the desk. Otherwise there were no embellishments. Inside the desk were some loose sheets of paper, envelopes, some paperclips and a very old Estabrook pen. Lachlan sat down to think.

He didn't feel comfortable in this town, this seat. He didn't know if he wanted to stay on, if the position were offered to him. But one way of testing out the fiber of a community was through the youth, with whom he felt easiest anyway. He figured, through the talk session idea he could gauge whether these were his sort of people, or dyed in the wool conservatives, as the parents would react to his idea quickly. He rubbed the fatigue in his eyes, then drew out of his back pocket a slip of paper with a poem by George Meredith typed onto it. It was a task he set himself daily, memorizing a poem. That is, when he was lonely; when he was not, he let it go.

After a three month period, Lachlan might or might not be asked to stay on in Ashville. The decision would be made by the Bishop and the people in the parish. There was no assistant. The parish was too small to warrant one. Most of the Episcopalians flourished in other parts of the State or in former mill towns along the river. This town was primarily Congregational with a smattering of Roman Catholics who drove north, on Sundays, to another town for Mass. There were only about two thousand people in the Town of Ashville.

Lachlan had been the assistant to a lazy Rector in Bridgeport. He had been energetic there, though he hated that city, and had been responsible for bringing many young people closer to the life of the Church. Lachlan preferred working in an urban environment, feeling he had a better defined purpose there, among poor people and corruptible youths. He didn't like this bourgeois community at all, but had to come on command, when Father Steele killed himself.

Bourgeois was a word he used to describe a state of mind, rather than a way of life. After all, certain material comforts were essential to all people living in a particular time and place; the necessary comforts corresponded to the particular place. He did not begrudge people their cars, pieces of property, or wall to wall carpeting. It was the state of mind that riled him, made him anxious. In some ways, he could imagine why Father Steele killed himself out here, and that made him long for an end to his three-month time period.

The state of mind that terrified him, in fact, was that of his congregation here. It was individualism carried to the extreme. Misanthropy prevailed. Irritation with error. Disgust at the workings of flesh. Although those he had met so far occasionally expressed a liberal attitude, he knew, sensed, if pushed, the person would react badly to change. These people lived here in order to avoid other people.

Lachlan, for his part, felt comfortable in base surroundings. When a baby was crying during his sermon, he was happy. When people were moving around during the service, he was happy. When people whispered, talked, coughed, gurgled, farted, he was happy. When people slouched, wore dirty shoes, lounged in the aisles, laughed, he was happy. He far preferred lunch in a dirty deli, crowded with dirty strangers, than lunch in the Ritz or Howard Johnsons. Among awkward, loud-spoken, rude, and restless young people, he was happy.In a poor neighborhood, where people wandered about mad, vomiting, pissing and shouting, he was happy.

He felt he would grow an ulcer in Ashville. The silence and cleanliness would drive him to drink.

So on Friday he drove to Boston to drink. He told the secretary at the Rectory, Adele, that he would be going home every Friday, which was his day off.

"Take care of things when I'm gone," he told her.

And he threw his things in the back of his old car and set off for home in Boston.

Back in Ashville, Saturday, Lachlan lay on his bed. A whacking hangover he ascribed to cigarettes, rather than drink, as he could dispense with nicotine faster than drink. His was a small bedroom in the parish house. Busy pink wallpaper and chintz curtains. His clothes, papers, books littered the room. It was a space intended for an assistant to the Rector, or for a guest. The actual Rectory was a red saltbox, built in 1784, and now empty.

"Father Steele's brother called, while you were gone," Adele, the secretary, told Lachlan on his return. "There will be some delay on clearing out the Rectory. Maybe a month."

"That's all right with me," said Lachlan.

"They say there was a ghost in that house already," Adele went on, folding her arms, "A restless spirit left over from the 19th century. Some kind of murder. Maybe, now?"

"Another ghost?" he suggested.

"Well, I don't really believe —"

"No."

He left her, fast as he could, to lie down. Eyes closed, he thought about Boston. A dark city, or one he shrouded in a half- light, whenever he saw it, or thought about it. As if he squinted the whole time he was there, and only opened his eyes outside its borders. He had returned to other places he had lived, when younger — to old apartment buildings, his house at Harvard, a summer cottage — and when he looked at the building, this same sensation arose. Windows appeared to squint back at him, like cloudy mirrors, a reflection of himself. How did I live there? he wondered. Was I half-blind, or in some pain?

He thought of himself as a happy person, so it was disturbing to turn back and see an image of himself which was shuttered, gloomy. Even sinful. But there it was. He didn't want to return to Boston, where his mother would dominate his life, and past acquaintances and friends viewed him in a larger perspective than he liked. "A poet and a rake," his brother Tom had called him. Lachlan smiled, nonetheless. He was being over-sensitive,

the hangover. "Some people's lives are a series of reincarnations," Tom had said late last night and hoped his own was one
of them.

Lachlan did not believe in reincarnation, although sometimes
he nurtured a supernatural vision of birth as an offspring of
death. A birth was sparked, ignited by the little explosion of
energy following a death somewhere. He didn't believe that a
person changed very much, while alive, either, unlike Tom, but
that those whose lives were 'a series of reincarnations' were
phoneys. Phoney was a word he used alot, being one of those
whose lives were directed by a reading of *The Catcher In The
Rye*. J.D. Salinger was the greatest influence in his life. After he
read the book, at sixteen, he would never feel that he was
unusual again.

He marched on Washington, sang freedom songs, travelled to
Selma, Alabama, worked in rehabilitation centers for junkies;
but he never went to jail or wanted to. His appetites were much
too important to him, and having an addictive temperament
himself, he was always sympathetic to other addicts and guilty
people. Still, jail was the limit.

For Lachlan the Creator dwelled in the rear of those whom he
faced, a presence hovering around the waist and buttocks. The
Creator steered a person forward, like two hands on the waist of
a toddler. There was not a living body which lacked this invisible but forceful prop. Even the most vile person (and Lachlan
was very critical) had access to the Creator. It was the head
which caused problems. The brain, an oversized lump, caused
people to act cruelly, selfishly. Children, Lachlan believed,
knew exactly as much as he did about the universe and its
significance. But his brain, growing in size, developed a set of
Dada-like perceptions, which led him to question the value of
life.

He went so far with this thought as to believe that spiritual
development ceases at age seventeen, if not before.

"Our task, as adults, is to sustain the vision we had as youths. If we can see through the eyes of our children, what we see will be much better and much worse than what we see ourselves, and it will be much closer to the truth."

One of his old sermons. He would pull it out, he decided, and use it again, here, the following morning.

Wednesday at four was choir practice. It was a bitterly cold day, overcast and windy. The interior of the Church was warm. Lachlan, in big boots and jacket, slumped in the back pew to listen to the music. The Town clerk played the organ, a slight woman, straight as a gate. They were doing *Brightest and Best,* one of Lachlan's favorite hymns.

Kathy Johnson (he remembered her mother's new name was Rockefeller) sang the first verse very prettily; then all the round white faces joined in for the rest. Lachlan was reminded, seeing her, of her kleptomania, and of a tea he had to attend. Would he dare smoke? He had to sympathize with her conflict; she was, on the surface, the epitome of piety. She would probably commit a worse crime still, and the papers would say what a good girl she had always been, so quiet and modest, and she sang in the church choir! This was how those accounts of suburban murders always went. The accused had pulled the wool over everybody's eyes.

Now Adele entered the Church with a big bunch of orange mums for the altar. She was a crumpled middle-aged woman, whose suspicion towards Lachlan had melted under his charm. She paused to whisper.

"Someone I never heard of called you — a long name. She said she wanted an appointment with you, but I said she'd have to call you back this evening. I didn't know your schedule."

He told her, assuringly, that he would soon have a calendar for her, and she bustled down the aisle to do the flowers. Lachlan stood and looked up at the choir, waving to Kathy. She raised her hand quickly, then dropped it and her eyes. He was beginning to feel better about Ashville, his mood expanding with the affection of the people.

Eight o'clock Tuesday Kathy listened to her Mom and Randy.
  "I can drink what I want," he said, "I make the money."
"And I babysit for your brats."
  "My brats!? I support yours."
"Don't worry, she'll be leaving soon."
  "She won't leave. After graduation, she'll still be hanging
  onto your apron strings and my wallet."
"No, she won't."
  "Want to bet?"
"I'll bet, okay."
  "Want a drink?"
"Sure, okay."
  "Believe me, I know these kids. They drain you of all
  you've got."
"She'll work, I promise, or go to school."
  "So who's going to pay for school?"
"I'll use my savings. She can get a job."
  "I'll believe it when I see it."
"She wants to be independent. She really does."
  "Here. Drink up."
"Thanks, Honey."
  "Like they say, you look pretty when you're mad."
"I'm not mad anymore."
  "That's my girl. We'll be okay. Just a few more years, and
  it will just be the two of us."
Mom did not respond to this remark. Silence fell. Kathy finished
climbing the padded stairs, on tiptoes, to her room. She sat on
her bed and tried very hard to lose her faith in a constant
creator. She tried, and tried, in much the same spirit as one who
tries to be healed, and isn't. As smug as a wart that won't go
away, her faith stayed lodged in the nest she had built for it.
Wouldn't budge.

Midnight on Tuesday Elmer stood inside Caralisa's door.
    "Thanks alot," she said.
"Good flick too."
He jingled his car keys.
    "I feel alot better."
"What about your old man?"
    "Oh, he'll be coming this weekend. I hate him. I feel as if I
    live inside his head."
"What do you mean?"
    "Like I occupy an apartment in his cerebellum. I just walk
    around in there, drive to the store, to work, to school, in
    there. I feel I am what he thinks I am and I'm only doing
    what he thinks."
"Weird."
    "It is."
"So keep him away."
    "I can't. He wants to see David."
"Don't let him."
    "I have to."
"You just think you do."
    "Really?"
"Really,"
said Elmer in a manly voice and let himself out the door.

Caralisa grew up in a series of ranch houses between Southern California, Arizona and New Mexico. Her father, Chuck, was a restaurateur; he owned a small chain of taco stands. He was a stocky, affable man; his father came from Genoa, had done quarry work in the southwest. His wife, Caralisa's mother, Juanita, raised the children pretty much on her own. Chuck was out on the road alot. Juanita, both of whose parents were still on a reservation in Oklahoma, was the one who Caralisa most resembled.

Juanita, dark, pretty and gay, played the piano in local night-clubs. She could play rag time, ballads, themes from great operas and current popular tunes. She would leave the children with various sitters and doll up for her nights out. She never had a lover. She was a little eccentric in her devotion to music, and shipping her piano from ranch house to ranch house was one of the major problems in their lives.

Juanita's greatest obsession was opera. Her hobby was the history of the Golden West. So, now, with her children grown and gone, she lived happily in San Francisco with Chuck coming and going as he pleased. Theirs was a happy marriage. Seeing each other rarely, and each being devoted to a particular occupation — Juanita to music, Chuck to money — made them enjoy each other thoroughly.

The combined effects of their characters made them produce two boys who lived on communes and studied agriculture, and Caralisa who was considered wayward, but was still loved. Caralisa could always go to San Francisco and be welcomed by Juanita, and she knew this, but she felt they were better off alone, without her. She was ashamed, really, of her past.

She had dropped out of Colorado University, had taken alot of drugs and gotten into endless jams, until she met Bob. Even though he had long hair and smoked grass, there was a basic conservatism to Bob. That is, he was domineering. Caralisa was more politically inclined than he, though he had opinions on every news announcement. Her attraction to the radical Left was based, in part, on her fear of punishment. Capitalism put an individual in a shakey position. You might slip and make a mistake by accident, then pay for it for the rest of your life. You might pay for it, not even knowing exactly what it was you did wrong! But the concept of collectivism, Marxist or not, included alot of clear rules. You knew, in advance, what you could and could not do, down to the smallest anti-social gesture; you could not, supposedly, make a mistake without doing it consciously. This was, for Caralisa, a blissful prospect.

When her parents saw her last, she was with Bob and the baby. The threesome arrived in a VW bug, their hair long and dishevelled, bandanas crossing their brows; and handwoven bags containing crumpled-up luggage.

"I have to take a shit," were Bob's first words to Chuck.

"Don't forget to flush!" Juanita called out, laughing.

Chuck did not like beards on young men. Bob had a beard. But Chuck loved babies and carried the wiggling David to the sofa to change his diaper. Caralisa, in her mother's bedroom, declared that Bob, then a free-lance photographer, was a genius.

"What about your studies, dear," kindly spoken, "and your own plans for yourself?"

"I don't have time."

"Well, come live near us. I'll help you."

"No, Mom, we're going back east."

"But you used to carry a book everywhere, and read, read, read!"

"Linear stuff is finished," said Caralisa. "What counts is visual, the here and now."

"Oh Lord," sighed Juanita.

The next day, Bob, Caralisa and the baby drove off again. It was the last time Caralisa saw her parents. In three years time, all had changed, utterly changed. Bob was making lots of money doing commercial photography; he had shaved his beard, renounced dope in favor of martinis; he had joined the Bicentennial Committee and had given up Caralisa in favor of an attorney with three children.

Caralisa, Bob had concluded, was a parasite whom he only pitied. As a champion of the feminist cause, he renounced Caralisa's inability to work and be a mother at the same time. He grew sick, he said, of her clutch. She leaned on him too heavily. Even after he steered her off onto other men, persuading her to have extramarital sex for her own benefit, she would come home to him like a penitent, begging forgiveness for an act he himself had encouraged! Don't you see, he cried, I don't care what you do.

"The best thing I can do for you," he told her at last, "is get out, let you sink or swim. Go on Welfare, whatever. I'll pay what the State requires, But that's it. You've got to grow up."

Then he took his girlfriend to Haiti to get the divorce. It was beyond Caralisa's powers to struggle. Ashamed, she slipped off to a shack in the woods. She had friends. People liked her, but she knew Bob had instructed them not to take her in. "She has got to learn how to survive on her own. Don't coddle her, for God's sake," he said. People listened to Bob; he was that kind of man.

Kathy told Frieda she was finished with shoplifting. Frieda asked why and Kathy just said she didn't want to get caught.

"But you never do," said Frieda, "I make sure of that!"

"I want to quit while I'm ahead," Kathy said coldly.

Only Lachlan and her mother knew she had been caught at Penny Saver that day. Her mother's response had been beyond anger; almost fearfully, she sent Kathy to Lachlan, saying "I wash my hands of you," to Kathy.

Frieda was desolate that Kathy would not steal anymore. She was losing her grip on her only friend. She begged and pleaded, but Kathy was firm in her resolve to 'kick the habit'. Instead, she was acting all saintly, and rushing around the class to persuade people to come to the Church with her on Wednesday night for the rap session.

"It's going to be a kind of discussion group, I guess," Kathy explained, "Only very casual."

"What will we talk about?" her friends asked.

"We'll have to see. The Minister, Lachlan, is super- cool."

"Cute too."

"He's gorgeous!"

"One of the great mouths."

"We have to get some guys to come too," said Kathy, annoyed at these digressions.

"Why?"

"It would look stupid, if just a bunch of girls arrived. Like we want to worship at his feet."

"Sounds good to me."

"Me too."

"Anyway, the guys need it as much as we do."

"Need what?"

"Whatever it's going to be."

Finally about fifteen people had agreed to go, a few of them male. Curiosity and boredom were the main incentives, though Kathy did her best to inspire her friends to expect a great revelation.

"Lachlan just seems like someone who tells it like it is," she said, "I can't explain it, but I'm sure we'll all get something out of it."
Frieda listened resentfully.
"I'll tell you what happens," Kathy assured her.
"Big deal."
Frieda lumbered off in a state of high dudgeon. Kathy, watching her go, had a slight panic. The compulsion to steal had not left her. She avoided going into stores, but glanced at people's purses hungrily. A vague fear that she might lose control of her faculties would rise in her. She was putting high stakes on contact with Lachlan to quell these fears and impulses. When the impulse to snatch something hit her, she quickly thought of him, his face which had a golden hue like that of John F. Kennedy hanging in the Principal's office at school. He would protect her, save her from evil and forgive her her trespasses, should they, by chance, recur.

But the night before Wednesday's meeting she had a terrible dream – That she was being caught again, outside Penny Saver, but this time by Lachlan!
He threw her up against the wall, shouting
"You're all the same. Pigs!"
She broke away from him and ran to a sewer hole. The lid was raised and she pushed it aside to climb down. But up came the head of Father Steele! And he was white as chalk, his hair ashy, he was smiling in a way he never smiled in real life. That is, with great warmth and kindness. Was it him, or wasn't it? It was, but it wasn't, and he wanted her. He grabbed for her leg, she dodged, apologizing profusely,
Sorry, Daddy, Sorry,
as his hands flailed and flapped after her dancing feet. She was, for some reason, unable, unwilling to run, but could only dodge, with skillful steps, his grasp, until she woke up.

Lachlan was in his element on Wednesday night. He had the kids draw up chairs in a big circle. One of the guys brought a transistor radio, and Lachlan asked him to turn it on, instead of off, as everyone expected.

"Do you think you all know each other too well, or not well enough to really talk tonight?" he asked.

"Not well enough."

"Too well."

Laughter and babbling responses. Lachlan stared into the ring of blue knees, jeans, and brown shoes, faces young, pale, some acned, some clear, some pretty, some not, long hair in various shapes and colors, and focused on Kathy, who sat apart.

"Kathy, what do you say?" he asked.

"Nothing. I mean, I think we all know each other pretty well."

"What do you want to hear?" one of the more aggressive boys asked Lachlan.

"What do *you* want to hear?" Lachlan retorted.

"I want to know if Karen dyes her hair," the boy said. Roars.

"Do you want to answer him, Karen, wherever you are?" asked Lachlan.

Karen raised her hand to show him who she was. She was blond and blushing.

"It's natural," she whispered.

"I've got an idea," said Lachlan, "I'll tell you about myself — where I come from — and then each of you tell me something about yourselves."

"Oh no!"

"No way!"

Gasps and protests. Blushes abundant.

"Then show me the latest dance," said Lachlan.

Giggling and hooting, some of them stood, turned up the radio and paired off to do some grinds for Lachlan. He lounged, watching, and lit himself a cigarette. In the back of his head he was afraid they might smell the whiskey on his breath, he had forgotten to suck a Cert before he came into the hall. Two girls, who were not dancing, lit cigarettes too, as soon as he did. Kathy sat quietly, her hands in her lap.

They all remained in these varying postures, some dancing,
some sitting, for the remainder of the evening. Lachlan tried to
dance only once with the Class President, a tall funny-faced girl
with a long jaw, while everyone clapped.

But when it was time to break up, she said in a loud voice,
"Hey wait, everyone. I think we should plan to talk next week. I
really do. I mean, I've got some questions."
"Okay."
"Sure."
"That's cool"
        "Thank you," Lachlan said to her, smiling, and he looked
        around for Kathy, to thank her for bringing everyone there.
But she was gone already. Lachlan was pleased with the way the
session went. He could foresee a Wednesday night when per-
sonal problems would be revealed, and the real amusement, for
him, would begin.

"I called that minister," said Caralisa.
"What for?" Elmer asked.
"To get advice, make an appointment."
"What did he say?"
"Nothing yet."
"He'll just say what I do."
"Not necessarily."
"You just think he's smarter than me."
"No I don't! But he has experience."
"So do I."
"Well, I know you're not as old as he is."
"I've packed alot in."
"I bet you have," smiling.
He didn't smile back. It was their fourth night together, he didn't dare touch her, though she would tease, like this, over a forkful of spaghetti, and make him feel maybe she wanted him. But he was as scared as a virgin!

"Some places seem to attract or induce violent events. Whether it's an atmosphere, an aura — who knows? But history shows that certain geographical and domestic locations bring on extraordinary behavior. Look at Southern California."

Kathy switched off the radio. A talk show on the Occult which was scaring her. In her dark bedroom, everyone asleep, now she lay down and heard noises all over the house. Little clicks. But no it was the rain, just starting on the roof, out on the pavement.

All day she had been dazzled by yellow leaves on black bark, pots of gold. The browns and reds had fallen, leaving webs of bark extending deep into the woods. Sudden explosions of yellow, bright as buttercups, made her feel it might be worth living after all. If pretty sights could only heal the soul! Her eyes would make an effort to devour the pictures before them, to suck them down into that area around her breastbone, where the soul stood and liven her up. They relieved her, only insofar as they drew her concentration off herself.

She kept getting attacks of diarrhea in class or out on the street and in her effort to control them, her sphincter contracted, causing a flow of energy to back up through her body into her brain, a delirious and feverish feeling, which she knew must be sexual and therefore embarrassing. The Reverend Steele had once used the term "exquisite pain" to describe the longing for God; it fitted her description for diarrhea just as well. There was nothing spiritual about the sensation; it put sex where it belonged, alongside defecation. So much for love.

So much for everything.
She let out great sighs, frequently, and involuntarily. Sighed now, in her bed, a cold gust of air. The clicking of the rain just six feet above her bed, and off to the left, against the window, brought back the presence of the Occult.

They said the Rectory contained a ghost. It was known to drift up and down stairs, banging doors, in the night. Sometimes it rolled fruit around the kitchen floor. The Town, being what it was, conserved all historical documents and made a big thing out of its place in the American Revolution. This ghost was documented, it was said, in records going back to witch-hunting days. Perhaps it was the ghost who drove Father Steele insane. This was a possibility that had not come to her, and now she wished it never had.

Not only did it frighten her; it tempted her. She imagined the Rectory at night, now, abandoned, empty, with no one, but two ghosts scuttling up and down stairs, bowling with avocados and pears across the kitchen floor.

"If I could just see them do it!"

She thought of rising, in her pink flannel nightgown, and drifting down the dark streets to the Rectory. Break and enter. She would be alone there, and, at last, free to feel out what happened to Father Steele.

"I want to do it!"

The compulsion to steal had broken through another artery, had taken a new track, this was how it felt. Wildly, she thought of Lachlan St. George, conjured up an image of him lounging, golden, in a flowered armchair, sun in his hair. Curly like Achilles, a beaming god of Light.

"He will stop me."
"I won't do it."
But this meant that she would do it. Whenever she made a resolution, she was compelled to break it. And she knew it.
"Help!"

Yin and Yang —
Yea and Nay —
Home is where the heart is? —
Will as Instinct —
How Children Survive Their Parents —
Thoreau, Tolstoi —
Health As A Luxury —
Psychology and Guilt —
"Someone Came Knocking At My Wee Small Door" —

Lachlan wrote endless lists for sermon topics.

Is Suicide Committed In Hope or Despair?
Death Is Natural.
Or Anti-Social?
Why Live?
Freud's Death-Wish —
Either/Or

He kept his sermons, envisioning a book someday. He would be the modern Emerson; nothing he ever thought would be wasted. He could see, in his sermons, a pattern emerging. His central theme seemed to be: How to connect the head and the heart in making a moral choice.

Is Morality Dead?
What Is Morality?
Where Have All the Flowers Gone?

First he had to answer these questions. And, for himself, the question his mother raised.

Does A Minister Have To Marry?
Must A Man Be What He Seems To Be?

Lachlan had never exactly understood why people get married. Of course he frequently married them himself, and advised them beforehand, and counseled them when divorce was imminent. He was good at those occasions. And he had no doubt that marriage was a sacrament, and once you did it, you'd better do your best to stick it out. But he still couldn't, deep in his heart, grasp exactly what it was that made a man and a woman desire to chain themselves to each other for life.

He did not, for one thing, view sex as a reproductive activity, but as a healthy activity, so long as no one got hurt in the process. He had made alot of mistakes in his day. Had fallen for various women whom he didn't, in any deep sense, love. But they were just that — mistakes; not sins, or symptoms of weak character.

Matrimony, monogamy and monotony were synonymous in his mind. He couldn't help it. He didn't like the idea of entering, freely, into that trinity. However, there was a vaguely degenerate quality developing in his actions these days. Aging, he assumed, was taking the savor out of the salt. What he wanted, now, was to try something new. To have, that is, a regulated life, wherein he could write seriously, in a civilized setting. His mother knew this before he did, as he perceived it, but she always knew everything before he did.

> That's the nature of truth, of course, he murmured, its waiting for you to be ready for it.

And then, one lonely evening, it occurred to him that marriage was actually a form of celibacy. Delight filled his hands as he grabbed for pen, paper and whiskey.

> That's why people get married! They enter a cell so they can sublimate!

He ignored the issue of procreation, as he had thought about that one before. So he tried out sublimation and celibacy as the twin offsprings of monogamy and marriage, and was off and running.

I'm really embarrassed, said Caralisa.

Don't be, said Lachlan.

I mean, I don't even go to church!

That's all right. Most people don't.

She smiled, relaxing. He was better looking than she remembered even from their brief encounter at Elmer's pump. For, even though her need for counsel was honest enough, she would not have come to see him if he had been wizened and grey. He had the kind of legs she liked on a man — calves bent like taut bows, muscular up to high buttocks — and a good long waist. Nice big hands and a healthy ruddy face. All man, but with a pleasing touch of feminine grace, good manners, she liked those too. She had already discovered he was unmarried.

What's the problem? he asked.

Well, she sighed, I'm divorced and have a small son. I live alone, on Welfare mostly, and now my ex-husband wants to take custody of my son. He's getting married again, settling down, he used to be super-hip, but now he's gone very bourgeois, if you know what I mean.

I certainly do.

She lit a cigarette and so Lachlan did too, happily.

Go on, he urged.

Well, I'm torn, because part of me thinks the orderly life would be good for David — my son — and having his father there too. But the other part says no. I mean, I love him, and I'd feel — well, lonely — without him — and guilty too. You know, the whole female role idea. I feel I'd be judged badly.

Lachlan frowned thoughtfully.

Have you been to a lawyer? he asked.

Oh yes. I've got custody now, but it would be simple to switch it around. He's got a lawyer, my husband, my ex, I mean Bob, and he's really pressuring me. He thinks I'm wild, unfit — all the things about me he used to like, now he condemns. Not that I'm wild, *or* unfit!

She laughed anxiously.

Lachlan noted the tight pants she wore accentuated pretty long legs, for someone so small. A smooth blue corduroy. Her blouse was peasant, hand-sewn flowers. An impression of beauty came from her face, but his impulse to hover there was squashed by the official environment of the parish house.

The thing is, Caralisa continued, it's a moral issue, not legal. And I'm very bad at fighting for my rights, I'm weak.

Lachlan raised his eyes to the ceiling.

It's a hard one, he said.

It sure is.

But becoming more common, of course.

I know.

Can I think it over? A couple of days?

Of course, she said.

Have you spoken to your son about it?

Oh no. I don't want him to get any more nervous than he already is.

Does he miss his father?

Yes. He adores him. Bob always comes to see him, twice a month, or more.

Okay, said Lachlan, let me think it over.

She stood up quickly, taking this as a dismissal.

You'll have to give me your number, he said.

There was a nervous shuffling around, by each of them, for pen and paper; he found them first, on the desk abandoned by the secretary, and handed them over to Caralisa. He looked at the phone number as if at code.

Where do you live? he asked the paper.

Out near the orchards.

It must be very pretty.

Oh yes, I love nature.

So do I. I might, next time, come out there, we could take a walk while we talk it over, he said.

Wonderful. There's a trail.

I'll give you a call — probably on the weekend.

She glided away, smiling to herself. Lachlan, alone, stood at the window, looking out, rehashing much of their conversation. He let out a solitary hoot when he recalled the words that entered his mind, when she said she didn't go to church —

"All the better to eat you with, my dear."

Where would I find historical records about this town?
Kathy asked.

The town clerk and organist replied, "In the library, obviously."

Is there a special section?

"Of course. Downstairs in the stacks. But you have to get permission from Mrs. Booke."

Mrs. Booke?

"She's the head librarian. At the desk. Are you doing a paper for school on Ashville?"

Yeah, I thought I'd do one of the old houses here.

"And obviously you've never been to a library before."

Obviously.

Kathy gave the woman a tense smile and slipped out of Town Hall, down the wide steps that faced on the village Green. The library was two doors away, and she started in that direction, carrying her school books, then stopped outside the door. An attack of diarrhea!

She looked at the door, as if it were a prison wall, unscalable. Her bowels were writhing, like a pair of serpents copulating on ice. No choice. She had to go in to see if there was a public bathroom in a public library.

She asked a huge woman at the desk, who said, "Yes, dear, right downstairs to your left," in a soft, small voice. Kathy pounded down the iron staircase as fast as she could, and dashed in the door marked Rest Room.

Safe inside the green cubicle, she clasped herself tight, and experienced an emotional revelation so deep, she nearly fainted. Her body, in its pain, was nothing but a thing; and she, at root, was no thing at all! *She was in the middle of nowhere.* She sat on the toilet, bent over, weeping for joy. That she was anonymous: nothing, nobody, nowhere; that she was not lost, but free! And she thanked God for her suffering, and how she was reduced by it to naught.

The pain, the pain, she hung there sighing for some time; and when it was gone, and she was done, she left the bathroom with a vocation.

FOUR

Caralisa, remembering portions of her own history, was sure she would never find the answer to her problems alone. Someone else would do it for her, as she told Elmer. And soon after she met him, she quit her job at the prison.

"I'm not doing any good," she explained, "The system is larger than me."

"It sure is'" he agreed.

Actually she was scared of the prison and of the prisoners. A faint bout of claustrophobia made her quitting easy. While having a job helped justify her existence, it also brought her into contact with men. Trapped in a green room with them, after several heavy doors had slid shut behind her, she did her best to talk about the American Revolution without blinking. But she was too feminine, and conscious of it, to pretend she was all mouth and brain.

Alot of male attention was not what she was after. But, as a man wants a dog around, so Caralisa wanted one man around. For protection and guidance. The world was not a safe place. A man at the gates of her house would howl and bite, should danger approach. Should she, in some way, become lost or confused, a man, like a dog, would lead her to the right path, leaping from side to side to scout out the environment. She would arrive home safe, which was all that mattered.

She had to justify this need in more ways than one. For her, measuring her needs against an abstract system of justice was a constant in her daily life, draining. She had to justify the most banal aspects of her time.

If she had forgotten to buy milk for David, she would give him soda, murmuring,

"Too much milk isn't good. High cholesterol."

Or, when she was in the mood to drive, she'd say,

"Wheels were the greatest gift to mankind."

Then, when she was in the mood to walk, she'd say,

"Cars have destroyed civilization. Everyone should walk, or use bikes."

And now, when she was feeling lonely and bereft, she said, "I've got to find a man. Without sex, a person becomes neurotic, anxious. Celibacy is unhealthy. And, besides, with the right man, I can keep David."

Trembling, Kathy went into Lachlan's office. Pepto Bismol was
her only hope for her bowels. He exhuded physical well-being
and confidence, tall and friendly as he was. He made her sit in an
armchair, while he sat on the edge of the desk.
    How are you, Kathy?
Fine, thank you.
    What can I do for you?
(He wondered if she had stolen again.)
I don't like to bother you, she said.
(The parable of The Good Thief came into his mind.)
    You're not bothering me, he assured her.
It's just that I have nobody else—I mean, my stepfather is all
involved with his boys, and my Mom, well, she doesn't
understand—
(He hoped she would not talk about sex.)
— I'm trying, she went on, to decide what to do with my life,
after graduation.
    Ah!
I'd like to do something for other people, you know, help
people, like you do, it must be, well, very rewarding.
    It is, when you *can* help, he said.
I used not to care.
    Why did you change your attitude?
I can't explain it.
    Maybe Father Steele's — eh — suicide?
Probably.
    That upset alot of people.
I know.
    But we're not talking about lots of people, he added pater-
    nally, we're talking about you.
Blushing: I hate to bother you.
    You're not, he assured her again.
Well, I'd like to do something in the Church.
    The Church?
Yes, like study theology, even be a Minister!
    Heavens, he said.

Well? Do I have a chance?

Hm, said Lachlan, It's hard to say off-hand. I'd have to give it some thought – taking into consideration your financial situation, where education goes, and your abilities.

I get okay grades, she said eagerly.

Yes, but you'd have to go to college first – get a liberal arts education.

I could do that – somehow – in a year.

Her eyes flashed, and he sat up straight, noting a small trail of pimples on her chin. He didn't know what to say. In the first place, he didn't like women being ordained, in spite of his liberal attitudes elsewhere. In the second place, he could not forget her kleptomania. Maybe this was a new form of madness. A latent snobbery rose to the surface of his mind as he contemplated her pale, inconsequential face, her absence of style in dress. If women had to be ordained, then let them at least be exceptional, outstanding, good-looking, from a certain class.

You might do better in Nursing School, he told her, I mean if you really want to help people.

I hate blood and things like that, she said.

Well, it's very hard, for women, I mean, getting into the Ministry. You couldn't come up with a more complicated goal.

But they do. I read about it, at the library, in *Time* magazine, they do get in.

Well, it's still a very touchy subject.

Oh.

She seemed to drop back from him, her eyes glazing. Her over-bright slick green coat, which she held around her, almost wiped her out completely. He stood up.

But I'll certainly think about it, he said.

Okay.

And in the meantime, you think about other possibilities. Like social work, say, or, uh, well, I don't know, let's think it over.

She jumped up.

Thank you, she said.

Thank *you* was the way he always ended a meeting like this.

Outside Kathy stopped beside the Rectory, looked around a few times, then slipped to the back of the house. There was a long rectangular lawn there, two pear trees, a back door and basement windows. She gazed across the surface of the house. The windows all still and grey, were impenetrable. Then she returned to the sidewalk.

"Hey, Kathy!" a voice called.

It was Frieda, wrapped up in a tentlike poncho.

"Where are you going?"

"Home," said Kathy.

"I just got the cutest earrings."

Frieda took a little white box out of her pocket and opened it to show Kathy.

"Did you steal them?"

"Oh come on, Kath. Don't be dumb."

"Well?"

Freida scrutinized Kathy's downcast features.

"What's wrong?"

"Nothing."

"Can I walk home with you?"

"Sure."

They walked along, the sky was heavy and grey, like the roof of the sea, imminent rain. Thanksgiving turkeys and Indians were pasted on shop windows. Frieda babbled about school and homework, blissful to be in Kathy's presence. When they got to Kathy's house, they sat in the kitchen eating saltines and peanut butter. It began raining. Kathy's morose expression increased, and Frieda said she had to go home.

"No, wait till the rain stops," said Kathy.

"But it will be dark then."

"So what? Mom will drive you home."

Kathy had never asked Frieda to prolong a visit, but now it had happened, they went into Kathy's room and shut the door. Frieda turned the radio on to a rock station and stood jiggling and gyrating in the center of the room, while Kathy lay on her back, on her bed, watching.

"Would you ever want to be a nun?" she asked Frieda.

"A nun!"

"Well, why not?"

    "I want to get married — have kids — "

"Why?"

    "I love kids."

"But after a while you might not love the man. You know?"

    "I'd still have the kids. To love."

"Love. Where is it?"

    "God is love," said Frieda emphatically.

Kathy lurched upright to look at her friend more closely than she normally did. Frieda's face was as smooth as a baby's, but not as moody. Her expression, even when suffused with the rouge of emotion, was placid, good-natured. Her eyes were bright little buttons; Kathy often thought of them as white. A milky sheen they were blue.

"So you just want to have children. To love."

    "Why not?"

"I don't know... I did the stupidest thing today."

    "Is that why you're in such a shitty mood?"

"You wouldn't believe it."

    "What. Tell me."

"I went to see Father, uh, Lachlan, you know, the new guy."

    "And you told him you were crazy about him, right?"

"Yuk! Shit. Wrong."

    "Then what."

"He's so pure, he's not even married."

    "So? Priests don't marry."

"Yeah, but he's not a priest, dummy. He's a minister. He could have a wife."

    "They shouldn't get married is how I look at it."

"Why not?"

    "I dunno. You can't serve God and Mammy. That's what my Dad says. He's a riot."

"He may have a point," said Kathy. "After all, Father Steele was married, and look what he did."

    "So what happened?"

Kathy drew her nails through her hair. "I made a fool of myself. Don't tell. I said I wanted to be a minister. And don't laugh!"

    "I'm not. Maybe you better be a nun instead. I mean, I don't think women can be preachers."

"No, you're wrong. But he made it pretty clear that it was a
stupid idea."

"That doesn't make him sound so good. If he made you feel
stupid. They aren't supposed to do that."

"I can't explain it," Kathy murmured, as a sensation of pain
wafted under her skin. As if someone had been mean to her.
"Certain things you can't put into words," she concluded.

"I think I understand," said Frieda.

Kathy felt profound shame. She recalled herself wishing for that
Elmer to love her, and it added to the shame she felt in regard to
Lachlan. It was like a form of alchemy, consciously adding one
kind of shame to another, all willfully, as if the product of the
process would be salvific.

✳

Elmer stuffed papers under the gridiron, on top of it, then threw on the kindling and logs. He did it with the quick efficiency of one who has built many fires, in much the same manner used by Caralisa making tortillas. The smell of chili filled the small house.

"I make a mean bean," she said.

A quick fry on the hot pan, each round tortilla; then she stuffed each one with beans, chopped onions and tomatoes, and a sprinkling of cheese. When the cake pan was filled up with them, she poured a hot red sauce over them and stuck the pan in the oven to bake.

"Mexican food is great for vegetarians," she said.

"For people who work in gas stations too," Elmer, deadpan.

David was rolling back and forth on the rug near the fire, singing *ohohohohoh*. When the fire began to blaze, he thrashed up into sitting position and jumped onto Elmer's back. Elmer, unperturbed, crouched, staring into the orange flames, while the boy pulled at his face. Drops of rain came down the chimney and fizzed in the fire. Then the phone rang.

"Oh hi," she said.

Elmer listened sharply. It was her ex-husband; her voice had dropped into something like a drone, dull and defensive. She called David over to speak to his father.

"I've got a big wheel," the boy said into the phone.

"A big wheel," he said again.

"A big WHEEL."

"A BIG WHEEL!"

Still the father did not understand and David thrust out the receiver to his mother, but she shook her head.

"Say something else, Dummy," she said.

"I'm not a dummy."

"Talk!" she shouted.

"Hi, Daddy," said the boy. And listened, unbuckling his belt and buckling it up again.

"Bye," he said in a minute and handed the phone to his mother. Caralisa made some quick agreement to something and hung up. She gave David an angry swat on the rear.

"Can't you ever concentrate?"

Ohohohohoh, rolling onto Elmer's back again.

Elmer glanced at Caralisa.

"Sit by the fire," he said, "I'll put him to bed."

Oh God thanks, she sighed.

Elmer helped David undress in the small bedroom set aside for him. There were not many toys, it was chilly. The boy wiggled and kicked, but his eyes stayed focussed on Elmer's face. Both wore similar expressions — wide, startled, newborn.

"Got enough blankets?"

No, said David, curling up. Elmer fetched another blanket from Caralisa and laid it over the boy. It would take him at least an hour to fall asleep, though he would not leave the bed or bother them. He would, instead, talk to himself and kick the wall, it was routine. Elmer, at the door, said, Give your mother a rest, she's tired, in just the same way his uncle had told him to settle down, a voice he had long forgotten. He tried to remember his uncle's face but failed, and, shutting David's door halfway, he experienced a chill like a shock in his spine.

Cold? she asked.

No.

Sometimes I get so mad, I could kill.

That's okay.

No, it isn't.

Did you see the minister?

Yes

What did he say?

Nothing. He's going to think about it.

Oh yeah? said Elmer with deep disapproval.

Anyway, Bob is coming down to take David for the weekend, so I'll have time to think.

Thinking won't get you nowhere.

What do you mean by that?

In the end, you'll do whatever you want.
     Hey, that's kind of mean.
Well, it's the truth.
Elmer announced his hunger now by getting up to set the table.
She watched him laying out plates and napkins, and noted the
lines of his torso under his flannel shirt and Levis. A good solid
body, not fat, not thin. And his hair was nice, shaggy blond, he
was not self-conscious or vain. He was familiar to her now, like
a real friend, the way he used his hands and moved his body. But
so young! The look of a kid, still, surprised. He tried to act like a
man, giving her advice and fixing broken pipes, a window sash,
her car; but she could see he was parading his skills to impress
her. They were not familiar activities for him, those little domestic duties.

He turned, she glanced at the shape of his loins. It was by no
means the first time she had thought of having sex with him,
how it would feel. But every time it came to her, she felt awkward and old. Too old to be pleasing to him. He seemed to like
her in a family way, big sister, from the same part of the country
he came from. She stood up.
     "Sometimes I hate all men," she announced.
He said nothing.
     "You're really innocent, aren't you?"
I don't know.
     "What I mean is, you have all the power, but you don't
seem to know it."
His eyes, alarmed, settled on her lips, where he usually found
true emotion was most easily read.
     "Let's eat," she said.

✳

At midnight Kathy sneaked out of the house. She had never done this before! There was the moon, full, spreading platinum across the town Green. The clouds of November, blue-grey as bruises, trailed high in the sky. All the fragrance of the day had vanished, the air was odorless. Like walking on a silver bracelet, the translucent moonshine on the pavement. A few lights shone in the store windows, warnings to people like her, that alarms would go off before a hostile gesture. She planned no hostile gesture. Her thieving days were over.

She could see herself, in the plate glass, passing, bundled up in her shiny coat and jeans. One car slid by, but most everyone was sleeping. She passed the Church, where Lachlan must be sleeping like a heap of gold, and went to the Rectory. A quick spasm caught her, as one has, at times, approaching sleep; the word GHOST had crossed her mind more than once; and then the image of spirits travelling up and down stairs, inside.

She squeezed a pocket flashlight and went around to the side of the house, then the rear. A basement window was what she was after, one that would open in and down. They were all at ground level, and, sure enough, the first one she tried, with a nudge of her foot, opened in. She squatted and shone the light down into the dark cement room. Some cardboard boxes, an oil heater, a couple of folded chairs. Swinging around, she dropped down inside, easily.

A tingling along the outer edges of her skin wired her in.
    "Lead, kindly Light," she said.
She pointed the beam of her flashlight to the basement stairs and faltered. But nothing ghostly hung on the clean wooden stair- case. So she approached it quickly, prepared to climb up into the intimate center of the house. It should smell of particular people and events. But she plowed on, and there was the smell, thick and stale. Soft carpeting, and polished tables. A plate of butter was melting on the kitchen range. She opened the refrigerator

and put it in, taking stock of the foil-wrapped bowls, a carton of milk, half a pack of baloney. But the refrigerator let out a great light and she shut it fast, for fear of detection. She left the kitchen and heard a clock ticking from some room upstairs. She mounted the padded staircase.

"As you look into space, you look back in time," her science teacher had said. "That is to say, what we see in the sky is ancient history, and years from now, we will be able to read, right up there, the story of how the universe began."

ALLAH, *it is written,*
backwards on the forehead, she had seen someone do this on t.v. But lead, kindly Light. He hadn't even stuck around to hear her sing on Sunday! She was really mad at him again. She reached the top of the stairs and saw a big brown Grandfather clock, the source of the ticking. On its right was a room where two twin beds sat like docked rowboats in a pool of moonlight.

That's where he did it, she said.
Grief seemed to lounge in the doorjam, she had to push it aside to enter the bedroom where Violence lay. Her bowels were growing lax. She knew, right off, which bed was his. The other one had a frilly little pillow on it.

"Your hands are familiar," said Elmer.
Caralisa looked at her hands which were small, smooth, pale brown.
  "But I can't remember who they look like."
Some old girl friend?
  "I don't think so."
Hands are very important, she said, some people can judge character by hands.
  "I know. It was my mother."
Oh. What was she like?
Elmer shrugged at this perfunctory question.
You aren't much of a talker, Elmer.
  "Sometimes I get going."
But you're a good listener. She watched him move to the window to look out at the night. Bathed in a blue light, the moon looked positively wet, some kind of jellyfish. He could sense the winter coming, in that glare.
  "When it gets really cold, I'll head south."
For a vacation, or for good? She stepped up beside him.
  "For good."
Where will you go?
  "The Gulf of Mexico."
You lucky, she sighed and moved to the sofa.
He eyed her, going, sensing her unease in the face of someone's ability to plan. She put her legs up on the sofa, wine in hand. Every time he started to go tonight, she asked him to stay. He was not comfortable.
  "Maybe you should live closer to town."
I lived in the city for years.
  "You have lots of friends?"
Yeah but I have to be alone for now.
  "As I say, I don't think it works that way."
Don't be so restless, sit down.
  "Well, I should get going."
Have you got a girl friend? I bet you do.
  "Not really."

But you're a romantic, I can tell. She must be down south some-where, that's why you're going.
Elmer just smiled and leaned down to tighten the laces on his boots. Caralisa put her feet on the floor and her glass on the table. Why do you come to see me? she asked.
"Home cooking. Good company."
He stood up from his boots and put his hands in his pockets, jingling keys and change. It must be the full moon, she said.
"What."
I feel strange.
"How."
Like you're going to turn into a wolf, she smiled and stood. As she approached, he stepped backwards, knocking up against the dinner table, where dishes still sat, scraped clean. Do you really have to go? she asked.
"Not right away."
She stood near him then, gazing down at the fire. Although he had wanted to make love to her every night he had been here, now that he knew he could do it, he didn't want to. Something in the structures of their speech and motions rang false. It was, he realized, a pretty familiar situation, the usual one around seduction, and he hated it. The way men end women dealt with each other. You could burn along the edges, being touched or brushed, and still, the two of you, would operate through some pretentious activities. It was ugly.
"There must be a better way," he said aloud.
To do what.
"What we're doing."
Naturally she knew what he meant, and sighed.
I can't think of a better way.
"I guess it's been centuries."
Actually, not necessarily.
Her face was orange towards the fire, and he mulled on the way it felt to be himself. Disliking sex talk, ever, made him wish it was all performed unconsciously, so that the eighty-percent of him which now felt savage, would put the rest to sleep. To do and to think simultaneously was a burden. If they were really equals, it would be easier, brain and beast fifty-fifty, and no

imbalance. But his interior was as imbalanced as their relations to each other.

"It's okay," was what he said.

The examination of her form could sensitize him, as if his eyes were films exposed to light, and he looked her over, every detail, just to make himself plain.

Caralisa eyed him back and parted her lips in a watery smile, a fountain figure poised to spout. He put his hands on her hips and pulled her close.

"Whatever you want is okay," he said.

She believed him, and was glad.

Kathy listened for a ghost. Nothing. Then she tried to feel the presence of one with her senses. But all she could do was concentrate on Father Steele's empty, suicidal bed, as if she could perceive remnants of his death throes there, a black angel, a child's digging in snow, arms and legs splayed, energetic rubbings.

"Life gives life to the living," her science teacher had said.

Kathy moved over and touched the bed. Various objects in the room caught her eye and filled her with pity. Possessions, the chains by which he must have swung from the empty sky, were such trite grasps on eternity. She wanted to cry.

"Who can be quiet the longest?" her father used to ask, when her Mom and she were chattering. It was a game they would play; Kathy could always be quiet longer than her Mom.

Now she wanted a revelation which wouldn't come. She looked at the bedside table where there was a tidy stack of books, all of them worn editions. TALES by Nathaniel Hawthorne, WORKS by Paracelsus, ISIS UNVEILED by Blavatsky, MOBY DICK by Herman Melville. She memorized the titles, imagining herself reading each book in search of the revealing phrase.

A feeling of exhaustion came over her, she sat down on Father Steele's bed. Her bowels began to churn but she didn't dare look for a bathroom, so she had to wait it out, feeling it go through the delirious stage, Exquisite Pain, when she cramped over and it passed. She stood up, sat down, stood up, sat down again.

If she just had the power to make something happen! But the only reward for her adventurous trip to the house was an increase in her depression. She lay down, her head on his pillow, and reached over to open the drawer in his bedside table. She fumbled around, in the light of the moon, and pulled out a flat package of prophylactics, called Trojans. She took one out and tugged it open, stretching it, and snapping it back. Then she stuffed it and the packet back in the drawer.

She leaned up on her elbow and probed around the drawer some more. She came up with a tube of vaseline and two silver bullets. The vaseline tube was half-empty, the bullets were clean. She stood up and went to the closet. It was packed with black suits, white shirts, shoes, a rack of ties, and on the shelf, magazines. It smelled so strong, she felt a presence hovering in the darkness, behind the clothes, the GHOST! and shut the door, slam.

Now her bowels felt bad again. I'm getting my period, that's why, she told herself, but felt the atmosphere of the room squeeze in on her, like two large hands, King Kong,a heavy odor. Gulping on a vomity feeling, she headed for the hall.

She would have to find the bathroom. There were three doors in the hall, all of them shut. She turned on her flashlight and tried the first one on her left. A child's room, not even tidied up, some clothes on the floor and tinker toys, books. She shut the door again. The disorder of the room increased her anxiety, her sense of intrusion, unfinished business.

She edged, nonetheless, to the door to the right of Father Steele's bedroom and tried that. It opened into a large bathroom. She slapped herself down on the toilet, her flashlight raised. Beside her was the sink; across from her a bathtub and shower. The rug under her feet was shag, yellow. She shut her eyes, as the tension poured out of her, then, finished, jumped up to pull the handle. As she did so, she noted that the wallpaper was flecked with red. Red spots on yellow. And, on the lid of the toilet tank, was a chunk of grey matter. As far as she could see, in the pale yellow beam of her light, it was the only such chunk around, but the blood was speckling the entire room, like the pale freckles on a brown egg.

Yipes, she said, and fled the room, bashing her breast against the bathroom door in her haste. She tore down the stairs and headed, recklessly, for the Rectory front door.

Outside, the cold air hit her cheeks and crushed the sick feeling. She gaped up at the face of the moon, which gaped back its grey and awestruck face. The sidewalk spread out like a bolt of white material before her. No cars slid by. She bowed her head and ran; but not home.

Like wax the meek shall be melted, and the affliction of the afflicted shall fail. Maketh, leadeth, restoreth, feedeth, preparedst, anointedst, hill and holy, king of glory, I do fear, I will. Imagine a mischievous device! My strength is in the dust with the dogs. Imagine my bones moving among my garments! There is no one to help me, not my mother's belly, not my mother's breasts. No father. I may tell all my bones, Trouble is near. They will trust and crawl and deliver and crawl and will be confounded. Blessed, said the Lord, be the glory of this place. And I went to him in bitterness. Thou shalt drink, he said; thou shalt eat, he said; thou shalt bake barley cakes, with dung, he said. Imagined, exalted, intended, inhabited. My heart is melted in the midst of my bowels. I am a worm, without bones. Out of joint. Abhorred. Despised. Worshipped. And his countenance shall not be moved. The people shot out their lips and laughed. The power of the bell was enfeebled. I will fear, I will. Tongue and nostril, I am powered out.

✻

Slowly the morning light developed on Elmer asleep. Naked, exposed. Caralisa was beside him, though not close, and she viewed him as if he were an uncompleted statue, stone emerging from stone, form attempting to break from element. No body, observed so objectively, could be beautiful. She felt no love, and its absence made her nauseous. She crawled further away from him, appalled.

But sex is healthy, she told herself, and I've gone so long without it, I was beginning to fall apart. It was natural!

Love, she knew, was instantly recognizable, and she recognized nothing here. "A learning experience," she rationalized, "I had to remind myself what really counts." but she knew, at heart, she shouldn't have done it — knew it, because she could do it again. And again.

Behind her, David stood at the door. For a minute, he hovered, staring, then went into the livingroom and turned on the television. At the sound of it, Caralisa whirled around. Then she leaped out of bed, and, grabbing her bathrobe, entered the livingroom. She shut the bedroom door behind her.

"How long have you been up?" she asked. He shrugged.

"It's too early for cartoons. Go back to bed."

I'm hungry, he said.

"Jesus Christ."

She rushed to the kitchen and dumped cereal and milk into a bowl, smacking them down on the table. Isn't it a school day, he asked her.

"Yes. I'll get dressed. Eat."

He watched her face with an expression of wonder, then dove into his bowl of cereal.

Caralisa, in the bedroom, started for her clothes, but Elmer reached up on his elbow and out, for her.

"Stay here," she snapped. "David's up. And don't come out til we've gone. I don't think he knows you're here."

He'll see my car.

"I'll say it broke down."
She was whispering, urgently, her face was a rosy mask of terror. As she leaned down to put on her panties, Elmer reached out and slipped his hand between her thighs. She leaped away.
"Don't."
I'll be back tonight.
"No, no, call," she said.
Look at me, kiss me.
"I can't, I have to run."
Then I'll wait here, he smiled to himself. She rushed from the room and started water boiling. Her gestures were quick and spastic; she glanced anxiously at David who was obedient and self-contained over his bowl. When she took him into his room to dress him, he stood silent, and only said, "Those are dirty" of the clothes she put on him.
"That's okay, it's too cold to fool around," she said.
Worn socks, worn shoes she leaned down to tie. And a surge of guilt came over her, for him, his cold spare bedroom, his Thrift Shop clothes.
"Daddy's coming this weekend," she said.
I know.
"He might buy you some new clothes."
She flicked on the television for him, cartoons, and slurped down some lukewarm coffee, before driving him to school.

Elmer was still in bed when she returned.

I thought you'd be gone! she cried.

I called in sick. What's wrong?

I'm tired, obviously, and don't want David to know.

Did he ask about my car?

Yes, and he made no comment when I told my lie. So. But you have to be careful around children.

I'm sorry, I know. Especially with his father the way he is. Come on. Lie down. Take a nap.

I can't sleep during the day.

Then just lie down.

She contemplated his energy, and yawned. His chest was smooth, muscular, a pale gold.

Come on, said Elmer again, and put out his hand.

Oh all right.

Caralisa stripped to her underclothes and climbed back into the space she had left. She turned her back on Elmer and shut her eyes. She knew everything that was going to happen, and instinctively chose not to see.

Elmer said, I'd like you to consider coming down south with me. You and David.

Mm. What for?

I'll take care of you. We can have a great time travelling.

Maybe.

Good.

He put his hand on her hipbone and began to explore. He was talking about Virginia, the Carolinas, motels, and Creole restaurants, moving his hand from place to place as if it were the very vehicle for the trip he described. Caralisa was reassured, responsive, the more delectable his descriptions became.

That sounds good, great, heaven, she murmured.

And the time passed fast till noon, when they heard the very distant churchbells chime. On the twelfth ring, Elmer climbed out of bed to dress.

Yeah, you better go, she said, heavy-lidded and smiling.

I'll call you later, okay?

Sure, fine.

Think about — well, think hot sauce, he said, Hot sauce and shrimp.

Mm, yeah.

He went to the door and left with a kind of utilitarian stride, which made her feel her exhaustion was immoral.

Elmer did not go to work at all that day. He imagined that Caralisa was sleeping, and took off for the next town. He made the rounds, there, of car dealers — Ford, Volkswagon, Toyota — looking for a van to drive south in. He wanted something large, big enough to comfortably hold himself, Caralisa, David and all their belongings.

He had the money in savings to buy a van outright, and when he saw what he wanted, back at the Ford dealer, he went ahead and signed all the papers, trading in his Mustang. It was late afternoon, too late to go to the bank and withdraw the money; so he called Caralisa from the highway.

"I bought a van," he told her.
"Good."
"Are you thinking it over?"
"What."
"About coming down south?"
"Yes."
"Any decisions?"
"Not yet. You know me."
"Can I come over?"
"No, please, not tonight, I'm bushed."
"Then when?"
"Call me tomorrow, okay?"

When she hung up, Caralisa rushed over to the sofa and threw herself down beside David, planting her head on his small knees. He was watching the Four O'clock Movie, Gene Kelly, *Singing in the Rain*. He put his fingers in her hair, and they watched the show together, then another, after supper. She wrapped a blanket around the two of them, warmed, too, by his mild manner, and the way he kept kissing her.

*

The Wednesday night talk session had stirred up some parental reaction. Just as Lachlan had expected, several parents were openly hostile and called him to express their concern.

"It would be one thing if you were discussing Church ritual, like the eucharist or confession, which they need to know about. But it's another thing altogether to have them do the bop in the parish house and practice Sunday Supplement psychology on them."

"We didn't get into psychology," he said.

"But it's obvious that this is what you plan to do, and what they want you to do."

"If they want me to do it, there must be some need for it then," he said.

"They're very vulnerable. We all fear the new cults springing up around us. You know what I'm talking about. Maharishis, gurus, yogi. Look what happened to Father Steele after he practiced transcendental meditation!"

This spokeswoman for the anti-talk session movement was the type Lachlan despised. She was very rich, horsey and tight-lipped, wore Liberty blouses, A-line skirts and cashmere sweaters with a gold pin on her breast. She drove a shiny station wagon and organized committees which were always *against*, rather than for, some particular issue. He despised her type, but his defender in this matter was exactly the same type, wore the same hair style and clothes and drove an identical car. His defender said:

"I think it's just what the doctor ordered. The children have been traumatized by the suicide. They don't want to go to Church anymore. A session, like this, will bring them back, relax and reassure them."

So the phones and kitchens in Ashville hummed and rocked with debates, regarding the rap session and Lachlan. Most were against him, he was suspiciously handsome and hip, an obvious liberal type from Boston, and unmarried to boot.

He was finally given the go-ahead on one more meeting, after which they would decide, as a congregation, if the sessions should continue or not. Lachlan was upset. He wanted to get out of that town as fast as he could. Every day there confirmed his mother's insinuations about respectability. As long as he was single, he was suspect.

At the second meeting, all the same faces appeared, except one. Kathy was absent. She had been absent from choir practice too, though no one called to say why.

"Does anyone know where Kathy Johnson is?" Lachlan asked.

"She was in school today," they told him.

"Well then, she can't be sick."

He gazed around at the people sprawled on chairs and the floor and instantly sensed they had been brainwashed by their parents. No radio. Subdued expressions, a faint impression of anxiety that was absent before.

"You all seem very quiet," he said.

"Well," said a long-haired boy, "We don't know what you want us to talk about."

"Well, how about, uh, religion?"

"What about it?"

"Is it important to you?"

"No."

"Well, at least you're honest."

A quiver of laughter passed from chair to chair.

"But you must worry, sometimes, about the meaning of life, your life, lives?"

"I do," said a little red-haired girl with freckles.

"I do too."

"Me too."

Only the girls seemed willing to discuss the meaning of life. The boys looked bored, or embarrassed.

"Well, I worry about it," said Lachlan, "all the time."

A heavy boy with drooping black hair said, "I worried a little, you know, after Father Steele wasted himself."

"Me too."

"Oh God yes."

"Well no wonder."

"A kid in our class, junior year, killed himself. With a gun, the same way."

"Billy Stevens."

"I mean, like he was the All-American boy type."

"Great at soccer."

"Nice-looking kid."

"Where did he get the gun," asked Lachlan.

"You must be kidding. All our parents have guns. This town is a regular arsenal."

"Are you serious?"

"Shit, man, my Dad doesn't even hunt and he's got a trunk full of rifles."

"That's right."

"Mine too."

"I guess Father Steele had a gun too, I mean, right beside his bed."

For some reason this remark made everyone roar with laughter, to the point of hysteria. Feet stamped, elbows bounced, cheeks reddened, tears poured.

"Wait a minute. What did I say?"

"It's just the idea!"

And they roared some more. Lachlan lit a cigarette, an act which served to silence them, as it signalled that others could smoke too. But now, to his relief, the room was relaxed, the atmosphere transformed from tension to a healthy confusion.

"Is suicide a sin?" a girl asked, grinning.

"Not to my mind. But the Church has a pretty strict view of it."

"Well, if you disagree, why are you in the Church, in the first place," asked a wild and long-haired boy.

"There's lots of room for disagreement, believe it or not. You don't have to stop thinking, or asking questions, when you are ordained."

"You have to stop giving the wrong answers, though," said the boy.

Lachlan looked at him quickly, and with some astonishment. The boy had the common teenage face, littered with spots and lacking in proportion. He was the most unruly looking in the bunch, more like a city hippie than a suburban rich kid; he was totally lacking in respect, or manners. Lachlan didn't like him.

"You can give the wrong answers, if they seem more true to you than the official laws of the Church."

"Why get into a system full of laws?" the boy persisted.

"Laws are necessary to society, to nature, to the individual."

"They're all invented. I mean, the Gospels have nothing to do with the Church. And I still don't see why a guy like you would be a minister."

"Did Father Steele fit the bill?"

"Yeah, man, he was crazy. He couldn't get enough laws. He would pick pebbles up off the sidewalk, and carry a rope around to tie up dogs who weren't on leashes. He would call the police at 3 a.m. if a car drove by. I mean, shit, he was made for the Church."

"Well, you certainly have a pessimistic view of the whole thing. But I'm sure you feel the same about all institutions."

"Not all. Anyway, I still want to know how you got into being a minister."

Lachlan glanced, rather anxiously, at the other faces for signs of support; but, much to his horror, everyone was staring at him waiting for him to speak. This arrogant boy was their spokesman.

"Well, my father was a minister," he began, "and so it seemed natural for me to follow in his footsteps. I am the oldest son. At first I resisted, and spent a good many years rebelling. I wrote poetry at college. I thumbed my way across the country and back again. I was involved in the Civil Rights movement, which you are all too young to remember, and spent some time in the South. But after a couple of years of this, I decided it was time to settle down, and I returned to Boston, when my father died, and went to the Seminary there."

"Huh," said the boy.

No one else said anything. Lachlan was blushing, or hot, his cheeks were red, everything he said sounded false and calculated; he realized he had failed to provide an answer to the boy. What was he doing in the Church? If he was just following in his father's footeteps, then he was, as the boy suggested, just a dog. He decided he must try again.

"Of course I always believed in God, and was always influenced by the life of Jesus. So it was not a dramatic change in my fundamental interests to be ordained, when I was."

"I guess, what Ronnie means," said the funny-faced class president, her fingers pressed to her cheeks, "Is that you don't look like the normal minister."

"In that case, I'm flattered."

"Don't be," said Ronnie, "I didn't mean that, anyway. I mean that, as long as you're a minister, you can't tell me anything."

"If I was a junkie, I could?" Lachlan said, openly cross now.

"No. If you were a monk or a priest, I'd listen, but I can't be bothered listening to a white anglo-saxon protestant minister. It's like you want the world and heaven too."

"Why shouldn't I want both?"

"Because you can't have them both. That's all."

"Who says?"

"Didn't you ever read the Gospels?"

Lachlan reddened, and stood up.

"I didn't call you all over here tonight to quarrel," he said.

"Don't be mad" a girl said.

"Ronnie's always like that."

"He's a Marxist."

"He attacks everybody. The teachers. The principal."

"It's his style."

"We're all used to it."

"Why do you feel it necessary to attack?" Lachlan asked Ronnie.

"Man, I hate questions like that. Psychology's bullshit. You want to ask us questions about ourselves. Why shouldn't we do the same?"

"No reason," said Lachlan.

"I thought maybe you were going to say something intelligent.

Like about what went down in this church. With the late Father
Steele."

"What did you want me to say?" Lachlan inquired.

"That technique's dead — fighting questions with more questions."

"I'm sorry," said Lachlan, "I didn't mean to avoid your
question. I don't think I've realized, adequately, the effect
Father Steele's suicide must have had on all of you."

"No. You haven't," agreed Ronnie.

Lachlan's eyes were sore. He sensed, on the fringes of his focus,
motions of attention on the part of the others. He leaned hard
on the back of his chair. It slid upwards; he almost fell. No one
laughed but him. He adjusted himself to a more casual stance.
Arms folded.

"From what I've learned, since being here, I gather that he
was unpopular, and knew it. He was not used to a community like this, but had come from the Bronx in New
York, where he was extremely active in social programs.
However, even there — in that world — he was a loner, you
might say. Shy."

Lachlan was making up alot of this as he went along. He was
inventing a story, that is, out of snatches of information, none of
which included social work, or the Bronx. He often did this in
his sermons; created an imaginary character, supposedly real,
to illustrate a moral point. He was good at it.

Was he a Jew?" asked Ronnie.

"No," laughed Lachlan quickly. "He was just an intellectual. He actually was a very good writer. Poetic. But not a
Jew."

"A poet? Wow, man, really?" Ronnie liked that.

"Yes. But he never showed his work to anyone. He was the
sort of person who lives a double life. One, the real one, is
intensely private. The public life is unreal, and rather ter-
rifying. The duality there could not have done him much
good in the end."

"But did he really believe in the divinity of Jesus?" asked Ronnie.

"Well, why not?"

"If he was such an intellectual, and all, you'd think he would have been an — uh — existentialist."

"Really? That's an odd assumption to make."

"Anyway, go on," said Ronnie, reddening a shade.

Lachlan lowered his head, a moment of floundering doubt, and then he said, as a complete lie, intended for consolation: "His father committed suicide too. And this, I think, explains it all. The children of suicides often repeat the act, when the going gets rough."

"Ha!" Ronnie rasped, sticking out his face close to Lachlan, "That's a lie. I did my homework on that one. His father is still alive!"

"Well — someone gave me false information then," Lachlan said with a smile which he knew was sickeningly false.

"Ha! Ha!" rasped Ronnie, and he socked Lachlan lightly on the arm. He left, making strange noises, ahead of everyone else. Motion followed his departure.

"We better go too," said a girl.

"Listen," said another to Lachlan, "don't worry about Ronnie. He's neurotic. His father killed himself a few years back. That's why he's so weird, I guess, about suicide."

"Oh, I see!" Lachlan cried with gratitude. "Of course."

"On the other hand," said a tall jock-like blond boy, "when Ronnie does his homework, he does his homework."

"As I said, my information must have been wrong," Lachlan murmured.

The crowd departed as a silent herd, leaving Lachlan to straighten chairs alone. His mortification was extreme. And some anger, too, directed, ferociously, at Father Steele. He tried to remember what he had said about the man, but couldn't. All he could recall, instead, were the facts he knew — that Steele was a solitary, who did poorly at his last post, and that he was a bookish type. He had invented the rest 'to comfort the children'.

"Ungrateful children of the rich," he snarled.

He knew it was the last such session he would hold in Ashville. He had no regrets about that.

✳

Elmer was parking his new Ford van in front of the town market when ·he ran into Kathy. It was Saturday morning. She was carrying a magazine and a can of Coke, about to cross the street to the Green. It was a wintery day, grey and ashen.

"You changed your hair," said Elmer.

"I just cut it," she said, touching her head. Her hair, cropped short around her ears and high on her neck, resembled a tight brown cap. This had the effect of revealing her entire face, opening it up to the public, as a nun's face is clearer than most when her hair is hidden away. Elmer was surprised at the size of Katty's eyes, a kind of stark and vulnerable look that wasn't there before.

"I think I like it better short," he said.

"You're the first boy to say that," smiling.

"How do you like my van?"

"You just bought it?"

"Yeah. I'll be heading south soon."

"Wow."

She glanced at him with open envy. Then they both turned and stared at the surface of his two-tone, brown and tan van, in silence, for a moment.

"So when are you going?" she asked.

"I've postponed it till Christmas."

"Alone?"

"I hope not."

She understood by this response that a woman was possibly involved, and it reminded her, again, of her stupid fantasies, fast to pass, about him, and love.

"Well, good luck," she said.

"Thanks."

They continued to stare at the van, and Elmer remembered not much about her, except that she was self-sufficient in a weird kind of way.

"I wish I could go away," she said, "like that."

He glanced at her wholly, and envisoned her riding in a tractor beside a father, both of them enjoying each other's company.

"I know why," he said to both of their surprise, "You remind me of a kid I knew, long time ago — on a farm. She went everywhere with her father."

"Why?"

"I don't know. But she always looked like she could take care of herself, as long as she was with her father."

"That's not me," said Kathy, "No fathers for me."

"Not even the one that art in heaven? I thought you were into religion."

"Yeah, that one's okay," she said with a reluctant smile.

"See? I was right," he said.

She nodded and raised her hand flat, sweeping it horizontally through the air, a goodbye.

*

As she did so, Caralisa opened her door to Bob, who marched past her without a hello.

David! he roared.

Daddy!

Caralisa stood back and watched their display of affection for each other, hugging and kissing, and looked miserable. She turned her back and burrowed in the refrigerator for an apple. Bob was a small man with long brown hair and round, languid features, a drooping mustache. He was neither outrageously hip, nor clearly straight. A kind of Laodicean look of one who could slide easily from one role to the next, according to his given goal. Pale, cunning eyes, however, which made it clear he knew his goals, at all times.

"I'll bring him back tomorrow night," he told Caralisa.

"In time for bed," she said.

"Sure."

"I can use the rest."

"Have you reached a decision yet?"

"No, but I'm trying."

"Well, don't take too long about it," said Bob with overt irritation, "I got married on Thursday."

"Congratulations."

"Her kids are eager to meet David."
"I bet."
    "We've got a big farmhouse."
"And two cars?" Bitterly.
    "Right. Joanne works, you know. A lawyer."
"You've told me that a hundred times."
        "I thought you might forget that some women do work and
    raise children."
"I bet she's rich."
    "She has some money. But she earns alot too."
"Wonder Woman. And *you* got her."
    "Don't be such a bitch."
"Why not? I've done all the hard work with David, for the past
four years, and now you come in, when all the shit is over — well,
fuck it. Fuck you."
    "Fuck you too," he said crossly.
She squatted to kiss David goodbye.
    "Here's an apple for the drive."
        "Can I eat it now?" asked David.
"No, save it, you just had breakfast."
    "He can eat it now," said Bob.
"Bye, Mommy," said David hurrying out the door to escape
them.

As soon as Bob was gone, Caralisa sat on the floor and cried.
Then she went and took a shower. Naked under the hot water,
more tears came. In spite of her hatred for the man, she was
scared of the complete loss of him. This was a secret, and
whenever she whispered it in her own ear, she experienced a
preternatural horror.

Prickling all over in a lather of foam, she thought about Elmer.
Help. At the very least he made her feel valuable, at the most a
real find. And although she could play with the idea of running
away with him, it was only a form of temporary reassurance. At
least, if push comes to shove, but it won't, I can split with him.

He was getting obsessive about taking her and David south with him, and she didn't want to hurt his feelings, or to make him mad. She was scared of people getting mad at her, and knew so little about Elmer — where he came from, or what he had done in his life — it scared her all the more.

I shouldn't have slept with him in the first place, she told herself, then in a rush took it all back. Repeated:
It's really unhealthy going without sex for too long. I needed it, I deserved it.

She left the shower and bundled up in her thick pink wrapper, anxious to crawl into bed and hide. With a towel in a turban on her head, she plunged to safety under the blankets and vowed she would spend the weekend alone. It was the moment destiny had selected for her to make up her mind about her child. She would face it head on, in solitude.

This time I'm going to do it. Then, with that done, I'll be free to move on to the next phase. I got this far, I can get farther again.

At noon, when Elmer called, she told him she wanted to be alone, all weekend. I have to make a decision, she told him. Bob says he wants a decision soon. Elmer protested, but for once she was firm, vocally. When she hung up, she shivered. The day was so cold and grim, the forecast the same for the next day, she couldn't imagine leaving her house. Solitude folded over her. She lit a fire and played the radio; then sat down and posited some ideas on paper:

1) I let Bob take care of David for a year or so, while I get myself together. I go to California & live with Mom till I get a Master's in social work, then come back and get David. (Bob will NOT agree to this, the motherfucker.)
2) I go with David and Elmer in the van south, and make Bob furious. Ha ha! But then what? I'll be stuck with Elmer. Drifting.
3) I keep David and we move in with Mom together, while I get my Degree. (Mom will drive me crazy. Bob will throw a fit.)
4) I

The telephone rang. It was Lachlan, or "the Minister". He said he would come out and see her at three. He said he had been thinking over her problem and had some ideas. She brushed her hair a hundred times, singing.

Lachlan arrived with his usual Saturday hangover, and much to
his joy, she offered him a beer, taking one herself.
    It's too cold to go for a walk, she said.
    It's horrible, but you've got a nice fire.
    Sit down! Enjoy it!
This is a friendly place here.
    It's a little rough, but that's okay.
Caralisa sat beside him on the floor, facing the fire, and lit up a
cigarette. He chatted about his trips to Boston, and she told him
a little about her life in that area, with Bob. At first it seemed to
be less of a visit for counsel than for company; but Lachlan was
dutiful and brought up the topic of her problem soon.
    I think, he announced, you'd make a mistake if you gave up
    your son.
Why?
    You wouldn't feel easy, as time went by, with the decision.
    It might look right now, under your set of circumstances,
    but they will change. They always do, thank God.
Well, that's true, but I haven't got a sou. I can't do anything to
improve my circumstances!
    Well, that's the problem you should think about, in my
    opinion.
Lachlan appraised her quickly, like a professional. She was just
his type. He knew that at once. A female pariah — removed from
his life at the Church — dark and extremely pretty. She was agile,
going to get another beer; he watched her small bottom from
where he sat on the floor, cleared his throat, trying to focus on
her problem.
    What sort of career do you envision for yourself? he called.
Some kind of social work, I guess.
    Why?
Well, my field is history, American history, but I want to apply
some of the feelings I have about this country.
    Like what?
She laughed, beside him again.

Oh you know, the classic Sixties' radical stuff. I went through all that.

So did I, he said.

It just isn't enough to teach, to talk about things. I still want to change things.

Absolutely, he agreed.

People have just stopped caring. My husband, my ex, Bob, I mean, is a typical example. All he cares about now is making alot of money.

Well, why do you want your son to live with him then?

Well, he is his father,and I can't help thinking a bit of security goes a long way, with children.

Of course. You're right.

Lachlan stood up to stretch his legs, far from bored, but saw that she looked alarmed, as if he were bored, or planning to leave. Quickly he smiled down at her.

Why don't we go out? he suggested, To a restaurant? We can have some real drinks, some food, and talk it over there. I don't have any more work to do today.

Caralisa ignited, jumped up. Are you sure? she asked.

Absolutely.

Your people won't be shocked if they see you with a strange woman?

That's what they want to see me with!

Besides, it's in the line of duty.

Of course it is, he smiled.

They were both slightly awkward, but she rushed into her bedroom to stare at her face in the mirror. She was embarrassed to see, openly reflected, her glittering delight.

They sipped manhattans in the cocktail lounge at Howard Johnsons. Lachlan, feeling comfortable, in the tacky motel-like gloom of the place, sprawled and sucked lumps of ice. He listened to Caralisa, who did most of the talking, balanced on two thin elbows across from him. She was elated. Real conversation after prolonged solitude made her feel adolescent. She could exalt the human condition; her personal history was an extraordinary story of survival. She wanted to tell it all!

Lachlan heard her at two levels. One was the spoken word — merely what she was saying; the other was what those words implied, about her character. Through two manhattans he was entertained and amused by her stories, her vivacity, and her shots of intelligence. She seemed to know who she was, her limitations and her abilities, and to be pleasingly lacking in self-pity or sentimentality. He always liked people who demeaned themselves.

"Can you believe it?" she would say. "I did it again!"

All her stories illustrated her foolishness. How she repeated the same mistakes, how she learned nothing from experience, how life itself bowled her over, how she stood like a ninepin at the end of an alley, watching the ball roll directly at her. She was laughing, at herself, at her resilience. She bounced right up again!

Then, before they adjourned to the dining area for dinner, she swooped off to the Ladies Room, and Lachlan, watching her go, was struck by a revelation. He would marry her! She was the One sent to him. ("In my distress, I cried unto the Lord, and he heard me.") Lachlan, who was impulsive but sensible, usually jumped to the right conclusion. Struck this way, he had no doubt. He thought of her face.

Hers was a universal face — round, childish, but womanly. Her straight coal black hair and olive complexion could have evolved almost anywhere on earth. She could be a tough Puerto Rican kid in Spanish Harlem, or a zealot in Jerusalem. She could, work at a loom in Guadalupe or carry a rifle in Cuba. It was a face he would never tire of.

On her return he insisted she order the most expensive item on the menu, a lobster, and he watched her rip at it, and suck on it, with a pleasing uninhibited appetite. She didn't mind getting grease on her fingers or defacing her own image with bits of lobster meat and butter. In fact, she talked about food while she was eating, allowing a circle of butter to gleam around her lips as she spoke.

I used to be a really good cook, she said, but now I don't have the right equipment. I would do seafood and vegetables in a wok — mmm! Good!

Lachlan, for his part, ate like a pig. Steak and baked potato, which he guzzled in huge bites, like one starved. He was known to have bad table manners. Even now his mother would lean over and slap the back of his hand, telling him to chew with his mouth shut and take his elbow off the table.

"People with a good appetite have a good nature," Tom always said.

And a good nature was, in the end, all that mattered. He recalled all the bright but irritable women he might have married. What he had wanted all along, unknowingly, was just this — an even-tempered woman, lacking in ambition. Bliss flooded him! He wanted to say what was on his mind, directly to her, but held his tongue. And as soon as he held his tongue, he wanted to leave her, to be alone, to savor his revelation privately. If he must be restrained, why hang around?

"What's wrong?" she asked. "Am I boring you?"

"Not at all!" sitting up straight.

"You look distracted — or something?"

He smiled, "I have to give a sermon in the morning."

"Oh God. I forgot."

She blushed into a steaming cup of tea.

"It's all right. Can we meet again tomorrow?" he asked.
    "Tomorrow?"
"In the afternoon?"
    "Well — sure!"

He paid the check, and helped her climb into her coat. He was aware that he was rushing, but his head was rushing too, he was impatient, now, to move, to get home and brood. Driving her home, he talked about her problem again, just to bring the night around full circle, to smooth it out like a tablecloth on an altar table.

> "Don't make any decisions about your little boy yet," he said, "or do anything you might regret. I know how eager you must be for a resolution to this situation — but it will come. Whenever you push a conclusion, I've discovered, things go wrong. Patience works wonders. Really."

She nodded earnestly at these words of his. Through drinks and dinner, she had forgotten he was a minister. Now she wondered how many times she had said Jesus, shit, fuck, or God. She shuddered in her coat. What was she allowed to say? Was it all right to say Jesus and God, instead of Gee and Gosh? The drinks had gone to her head! She was sure she had cussed more than once, but she couldn't remember in what fashion. And the worst of it was, now that she was aware of his status, dirty words were irresistible. She didn't dare open her mouth, for fear a stream of expletives would pour out.

> "Your little house looks rather lonely in the night," he said.
She nodded, her lips tight.
> "Well I expect it's just a temporary nest," he added, parking beside her car.
She jumped out. He followed and walked her up to the door.
> "Goodnight, Caralisa."
"Thank you," she blurted. "See you tomorrow!"
> "Probably around three," he said.
She flew inside, slamming the door.

Lachlan, walking back to his car, was aware of the sudden shift in her mood and worried that he had been too forward, asking to see her again the next day. He could hardly expect to lecture her on patience, successfully, and then overstep his bounds in a simultaneous leap. He decided to practice what he preached, the following day, to be more reserved and paternal. He wouldn't drink, but just have a cup of tea, and then leave.

FIVE

"Each person has an equal capacity for doing good, and for doing evil. When in a state of conflict, we might not even realize that this is the strain we are feeling. Between good and evil. Between yes and no. Between I don't know. Once we realize that the conflict is innate, that the negative is innate, as is the positive, we can begin to make correct choices."

Thus spoke Lachlan from the pulpit.

Kathy, seated on the steps of the church, heard him. But just as geometry is not algebra, her feelings did not correspond to his words. The correlation was obscure. She thought of a map of the moon she had seen. Amazing names the moon's spots were given! Barren it might be, but the names for its places were all emotional. The Ocean of Storms, the Sea of Tranquility, the Sea of Nectar, the Sea of Clouds, the Marsh of Decay, Seething Bay, the Sea of Fertility, the Sea of Cold.

The face of the moon, painted in grey swabs, wobbled to life under these moody names. She wandered through these moods by chance, but could not control the length of her visits. If she happened, luckily, to find herself in the Sea of Tranquility, or the Sea of Nectar, she was suddenly pulled along, by celestial gravity, to those foaming and misty places called Storms, Clouds, Seething, Decay and Cold! The bad names far out-numbered the good, she noted. What an imagination had recorded the brain-gray sections of the moon, and given them moody names!

Her own brain was a portable moon. It held these desolate sections; her spirit was doomed to pass through them, daily. She said she had a sore throat, and couldn't sing in the choir. But, in fact, she just couldn't sing at all. Since her night out, wandering the areas around Ashville, after her trip through the Rector's house, she could hardly talk.

She could only talk after she stole a sip of liquor from the cabinet in the kitchen. Alcohol shot her straight into the Sea of Nectar. Her brain held a Sea of Nectar, just like the moon, but only waiting to be discovered by alcohol. The life-giving drink of the gods, Nectar!

Tranquility followed Nectar; then Storms, Cold, Decay.

She was scared. She imagined Lachlan preparing the communion table. Gold, red wine, candles feathering lights onto the curve of the cup. He was Nectar personified! A gold chalice, full of wine, rather than blood. He radiated happiness, sanity, moral health, all those qualities which spring naturally from goodness.

To be so good, and free of evil, even if he suggested evil was innate in everyone, was all she desired. For if she could *be* good, she would feel good. Alot of the time, she tried to remember feeling good, hoping that the memory would ignite the present into happiness, but it didn't work. She could only remember being in a state of misery.

Now she heard everyone inside stand up to sing, and she wondered how she ever sang there before – alone, so brave! If that had been truly she, where had she gone? Was she, herself, buried alive inside herself, or had she flown away?

Others laughed, talked whispered and sang; they lapped up the eucharist like an hors d'oeuvre. Not she; no more. No spiritual leaven for one as leaden with gloom as she was. Frieda, these days, was the only person Kathy liked to be around.

Frieda seemed to understand that the problem was spiritual, and not psychological. At all costs Kathy wanted to avoid labelling herself with terms like severe depression, psychotic break, paranoia, terms which made her want to burst open like a wounded melon and leap into space.

Frieda suggested things like, "You should say the Hail, Mary. I do, and it works miracles."
"Say it for me," Kathy instructed from the bed, where she sipped creme de menthe from a dixie cup.

Frieda had looked embarrassed, saying it aloud, but Kathy made her repeat it nonetheless, until she knew it by heart. She had to admit the words had a good rhythm — especially 'fruit of thy womb, Jesus' — and a good sound too. But they couldn't quite conquer the cycles of her brain. Kathy was tossed into the Marsh of Decay, no matter how many Hail, Marys she uttered.

Frieda bought her a rosary, made of pink and silver beads, with a little image of Mary dangling from it.
"Keep this with you always," she said, "and you might begin to feel better."

Obediently Kathy carried it everywhere. She would twine it around her fingers, deep in her pocket, praying for an end to her misery and anxiety, but it first grew wet with the sweat in her hand, then snapped in half.

Still she carried it around. Now, leaving the steps of the church, she pinched the image of Mary between her thumb and forefinger, till it stamped an impression there where her thumbprint would be.

"Don't you want to see my van?" asked Elmer.

"Not today," said Caralisa, "Sorry."

"Well, why not?"

"Bob is coming. Bringing David back."

"So?"

"I'll want to talk to him."

Elmer hung up and stood in the pay phone booth, staring at his van.

When he hung up on her, Caralisa was relieved. If she could just make him go away, either in a rage or in peace, she would be happy. Happier yet, if she could erase from her memory the entire experience with him. In the past she had depended on men to get rid of other men, for her. But now she would have to do it herself firmly.

A great excitement was rising in her with the approaching minister. She cleaned the house and put the few toys belonging to David on a shelf in a neat row. Touching his toys made her miss him and suffer a slow shudder of guilt. His divided life! – and something in the custody quarrel implied a sinister under-side: neither parent might want him, really. For the moment he was treated as a piece of property, no matter how coveted, he was, also, subject to disposal. She sat on the edge of his bed.

This is called facing the facts, she told herself. When she and Bob were together, still, and David was just a toddler, there was this feeling of the child as innate to their lives and flesh. He was simply there, rolling back and forth between the two of them. An offspring! But now, he was property, an object, and not so innate after all. She could take him, or leave him. She could actually say, I don't want to be a mother, and it would be done. She would be free. But what if neither of them wanted him, one day? Maybe this was his perception of the situation.

"He seems a little insecure," his teacher said, politely.

"Nervous. Unable to concentrate. Although he's very bright!"

To live with an insoluble problem was more than she could bear! An error she couldn't bolt from! And tomorrow she had to go to the Welfare office! She had forgotten! She leaped up from David's bed and filled a bucket with hot water and suds. She fell on her knees, scrubbing the kitchen floor. She was beginning to feel pressed, as if that higher city in her head were putting a squeeze on her thought process.

"I should never have slept with Elmer. I should go away with him in his van. I should just run with David, prove my love for him! I should never have come to this town. I should have said No to Bob, right at the beginning. I should go back to school, get a degree, be useful. I should get off Welfare. I should take a risk. I should cut men out of my life altogether!"

By the time Lachlan arrived, Caralisa was so agitated, she could hardly pour the tea. He was oblivious to this, being very nervous himself. Their conversation was awkward and repetitive, and he rose to leave, after an hour of unrelieved tension.

"Please," she cried, "Come back tomorrow. Have dinner! I'll cook. Okay?"
He hooked his hand on the door, tight, and nodded, Fine.
"Around six?"
"And I'll bring some wine."

She stared up at him, as if her eyes were straining to see the Sea of Tranquility on the moon's surface. He touched her hand, then withdrew, as if he had touched a hot dish. Lachlan banged out the door and tripped on a rock, outside, in his haste. She watched him stagger and liked him better.

The Welfare Department had a concrete building in a town called Centerville. An old mill town, where a river ran between red brick buildings and under a functioning drawbridge. Now a small city, Centerville had the classic Main Street holding all that the heart desired in the way of goods. Woolworths, service stations, Dunkin Donuts, cheap clothes stores, pharmacies, doctors, dentists and sporting goods. Encircling Centerville were pale green hills.

The Welfare office was pale green. First a waiting room, shabby, with crooked and wobbling chairs, plentiful ashtrays, and a counter covered in glass, through which one spoke to a grumpy woman with glasses down her nose. To the left of her, a door opened into a vast room, filled with people of all sizes and ages who typed, frantically, at small desks. To the right of her, a corridor like a European train, with glass partitions, trailed to conclude with a water fountain. In these glass partitions was a table, and a chair on either side of it. Once you were inside the partition, the door was closed behind you, and you were trapped there with your judge.

Caralisa got a middle-aged woman this time. She was very tall and flat. Her chest was flat, her dress was flat, her shoes were flat, her nose was flat and her eyes were flat. She wore a flat grey bun at the back of her head. The bun, Caralisa supposed, was meant to give shape to her flat head. She came with forms, at least five sheets of paper, and then another batch of old forms, containing old facts about Caralisa. She shuffled through them with great speed.

"What's your situation now?" she asked Caralisa.
"The same."
"Have you looked for a job?"
"Yes."
"You only have one child. You should be able to come up with something."

"I'm not very qualified."

"Everyone can find something."

"I'll keep looking," Caralisa murmurred.

"You can, you know, keep your food stamps and medical card for some time after you get a job."

"I know."

"Your ex-husband has been paying us regularly," said the flat woman in a flat voice, gazing up at Caralisa. "Most of them don't. Wouldn't he pay you directly? Can't you ask him for support, alimony? It would save you these trips out here, and us alot of paper work."

"He — uh — won't do that."

"Well, why not?"

"I don't know. He wants to do it this way."

"Of course it doesn't cost him as much as alimony."

"No."

The woman stared at Caralisa for a moment, then sighed. The sigh passed through Caralisa's head like a cold mistral, bringing grief, depression. She stared into her hands.

"Well, let's get on with these forms then," the woman muttered, and began to write.

Caralisa watched her hand darting across the dotted lines, copying from one paper to the other. She looked over her shoulder and saw three people passing, women, two black, one white. It might have been a parade of maniacs through the halls of a city hospital! Each woman had a face and appearance more terrible than the one before! Bedraggled, wild, middle-aged, toothless. And for some reason, each one turned and smiled at her, in passing. Not one of them had a tooth. Each one wore a heavy overcoat. It was one of those occurrences that, like an hallucination, terrify the witness. She stared, as they trailed away, and were followed up by three young white men, Welfare workers with spongy upright faces. The bright light and pale green washed over their whiteness as water over fish in an aquarium.

"Okay. Give me your bills. Oil, electricity, rent," said the flat woman.

Caralisa reached in her purse and pulled out a wad of old bills and shot them across the desk to the woman.

"Sorry," said Caralisa as the papers drifted to the floor.

The woman scrambled around the desk for them. Then Caralisa followed, falling on her knees to collect the odd paper. From her base position, she spoke to the face of the woman hanging down nearby.

"This is the last time," said Caralisa, "I promise. I'll find a job."

The woman's face, swelling as it hung down, rotated slowly to stare at Caralisa on her knees.

"You do that," she said.

There were two things that could knock Caralisa out of despair:
one was a new article of clothing; another was cooking. And she
was in despair, all the way home from Welfare and all the way
to the market. But as soon as she began to peruse the vegetables,
cheeses and fruits, she felt better. She was preparing for
Lachlan! She hovered over heads of lettuce, squeezing each one
for size and weight. David bumped around her legs, asking for
candy which she got him.

In the car she told him,
    "I want you to be a good boy tonight. A man is coming, and
    he works in a church!"
"What's that?"
She looked impatient, frantic, at the ignorance for which she
alone was to blame.
    "A church is where God lives. I've showed you churches.
    Those white buildings downtown, with pointed tops —
    steeples."
"God lives *there*?"
    "Well, sort of. His spirit."
"His spirit?"
    "You know. The part of you that lives inside, where no one
    can see. That's your spirit."
"Oh," he said, "I get it."
    "Good."

Later, David raised the subject of God again. She was squatting
while he worked on the top button of her blouse.
    "Is God a man?" he asked.
"Of course not. He's nothing. Like air."
    "Then what's so great about it?"
"Well, he made you."
    "Why do they call him 'him'?"
"Oh they just do that. I don't like it, really, it makes it sound like
he's a man. But he's not."
    "Oh," he said, "I get it."

He trailed her into the other room. She was moving fast, tonight, revved up. Already she had bread baking in the oven; it filled the house with a warm yeasty smell. Now she was doing a spinach souffle, salad, and had chocolate mousse chilling in the refrigerator. She let David set the table. He put the forks and knives upside down, as if people would be sitting in the middle of the table, facing the chairs. But she decided not to remark on his error, but change it herself when he was in bed. He was being surprisingly good, more like a friend than a son.

"I had a horrible day today," she told him.
"Why? What happened?"
"I had to see some horrible people about getting us money."
"Money?"
"Money."
She reached in a cabinet and pulled out a half-gallon of cheap burgundy, which she poured and swilled, now, quickly. David grabbed her leg, hugging her, and she spilled some wine into his hair.
"Fuck, shit!" she screamed, then covered her mouth.

She heard Lachlan's car outside.

After work on Monday Elmer went back to his place with a pizza. He was planning to study the triptich maps of the South, given him by the AAA. To plan his route. He had already told Sam he would be leaving soon, gave him at least two weeks notice. He settled down with his pizza and Coke, but he couldn't seem to focus in on the maps. The silence of his room got under his skin; he turned on some music. But the music and the pizza failed to enliven him. Finally he threw the food away, turned off the radio and went outside.

It was cold but clear. The sky was a shower of stars and a huge round moon. There was to be an eclipse the following night, he had read. Inside his van, he felt some stirring up of his juices, the smell of it, the sweet smell of success, brand new, and its large size, its sheen, filled him with pride. He had blown almost all of his savings on it, but then he had a regular checking account to carry him on down till he stopped to work again, down south, somewhere. He drove out of town and connected up with the main highway, heading north for about twenty miles, before starting back.

A numb pain the size of a baby's fist sat in his left temple. The driving helped, but did not relieve it completely. It was the closest thing to a strong emotion that he was feeling, and hurt. When he left the highway, he headed out towards the orchards. She had said she was busy. What's up, he had asked. I'm finally seeing that minister, she had said. At night? he had asked. He's busy all day, she replied.

The trouble with where she lived was that he couldn't approach it without being seen. No cars went down there unless they were coming to her door. He couldn't then drive down, turn around and drive back. He would have to park at the end of the road and walk down in complete silence. The moon was so bright, it might have been daylight, early morning, just as the sun comes up. He parked the car by the orchards. There was still a residue smell of rotten apples. He stood inhaling it for a moment, before setting off down the road, slowly.

Blue smoke, a thin trail, from her chimney and around the edges of the windows a smell of baking bread. Yellow light filtered through the faded chintz curtains on the windows. He could see, looking up, the colors in the stars — they were so bright — red, orange, blue. Sparks.

On a night just like this, in the High Sierra, Elmer had struck a man with the nose of his car — his old Buick — and had driven on, fast, after stopping only for a minute to make sure the man was dead. He was. Driving away, Elmer told himself he would have stayed if the man had been alive; but it wasn't his fault when he hit him, and so it was not his responsibility.

He had not thought about that episode, except briefly, until tonight. But now there was a smell and feeling to the air that was identical with that moment, a heady association, a smell of high burning, thin air, and the stars on his head, close as a crown. The ability to kill! Jewels in his hair!

He had a runny nose, though, from the cold, and what he saw in the window was giving him a sick feeling. Caralisa, David and the minister. Their manner was awkward and fresh, as if they had just met, true, but somehow they formed a natural unit, the three of them.

Caralisa was a full-grown woman and the minister was a man. The window ledge, where Elmer stood, was so high it put his eyes at the level of a child's, in relation to them. He only came up to the minister's fly. Caralisa was pouring egg yolk from one bowl into whipped egg whites in another bowl, her hands maternal and able, the way they moved. The Minister was talking down to David, like a social worker or the Messiah, his head slightly tipped, a glaze of patience in his face.

All were utterly unconscious of Elmer's eyes, at window level, watching, as members of an exclusive club are unconscious of the eyes of the servants. In this case, age and experience gave them access to a club he could not join. He felt himself diminish to the size of comic books and cereal boxes. They smoked and drank French wine.

He saw Caralisa eyeing the minister from behind, a look anxious to please and pleased by what it saw. His body burned in the ice cold air, the longer he stared, the baby's fist in his temple swelled to the size of a trout. He remembered her mouth close to his, her eyes too, as she lay on him, naked. He had no tender feelings for her then, or now, but something greedy and painful, like an appetite for poison.

He considered violence. Flinging open the door. Exposing her to the minister. Pulling down her pants. Before it was too late, and everyone had succumbed to a new game. He looked at the minister's car, parked beside hers, and imagined stripping if of its parts, so she would have to call Elmer for help, and the minister would be seen as he really was – useless.

Now the cold came back through the thin veneer of his skin. The very thought of cars brought relief with it, a vision of freedom and escape. He could always turn and drive away. He took one more look inside; she was leading David off to bed; and the Minister was smiling vacantly through a veil of nicotine, his fingers draped lightly around a glass of wine.

"Hypocrite," he decided, and started back to this van over the crushing leaves.

"He's a sweet boy," said Lachlan.

"Yes, he is," she agreed.

Lachlan stood and stretched, trailing her to the stove, where the smell of souffle and the heat were strongest. Two loaves of bread sat cooling, side by side.

"Ah, bread."

"Baking bread," she said, "is the closest thing to having a baby I know. It gives the same feeling."

"Would you want more children?"

"Oh yes! Only is lonely, as my mother used to say."

"What did you tell your husband yesterday?"

"My *ex*-husband. I told him I wanted to keep David," she lied.

"What was his response?"

"Angry."

"Still, you have custody."

"It will be all right."

She whapped the salt shaker with the side of her hand and it rolled to the floor. Lachlan, picking it up, saw her fling a pinch of salt over her shoulder.

"Superstitious?"

"I knock wood too."

"Superstition," he said rather pompously he realized, "is like prayer."

"How?"

"Well, it indicates a positive desire — that things should work out for the best. People who are neither superstitious nor religious are often quite destructive. They don't bother thinking about the future, or the outcome of their actions."

He plucked a leaf of salad from the bowl.

"I don't know how to pray," she confessed.

"The best way to learn is by thinking of your actions as expressions of prayer."

"That's interesting," smiling, "I'll have to try it."

"You never go to church, you said," chewing the salad he stretched for more.

"It wasn't part of my background. But I feel, often, empty — like

I'm missing something. I mean, I've tried Yoga and meditation, but they didn't apply to the moral problems, if you know what I mean."

"I do indeed," he said.

He was pleased. He had feared he would find flaws in her that would dampen his revelation. The day before he had been so awkward, he had arrived, tonight, with some suspicion. The after-effects of his suspicion were a series of pompous remarks. He couldn't stop himself from making them! He was testing her, in spite of his conviction that she was the One sent to him.

"All my religious education," she said, "came from college. I took a course in the Old Testament, then in the New Testament, then one called Comparative Religions."

"But you never were inclined to go to Church?"

"Oh sure. But I was scared of it, in a way."

"Well, we'll have to take care of that."

Smiling up from under, "What about a divorce? Isn't that considered immoral?"

"No! Not anymore. Why, you weren't even married in a church."

"Oh. Right."

She bustled to the table with the food. He followed, the bowl of salad in one hand, his other hand in the bowl of salad, plucking.

"I'm sorry. There's not meat," she said.

"It looks wonderful," he assured her.

"It's just so expensive," said Caralisa. "Meat."

Sitting down, she folded her hands in her lap, wondering if he would say Grace; but he didn't. Somehow this relieved her of all guilt in failing to tell him she was a vegetarian — a fact about herself she decided to conceal, as it would make her sound degenerate.

Dear Reverend
Dear Lachlan
Dear Father St. George
My Dear Reverend Father
Dear Sir
Dear Lachlan
              If I could only put into words
              It's hard to say
              I'm not good at
              I'm writing this letter
              Words escape

Dear Reverend St. George,
     You may not remember me

Dear Lachlan,
     I am sorry to bother you

Dear Father St. George,
     This is just a note to ask if you can help me. I feel like a
walnut!
              There was a little green house
              And in the little green house
              There was a little brown house
              And in the little brown house
              There was a little yellow house
              And in the little yellow house
              There was a little white house
              And in the little white house,
              There was a little heart.
That's me. How does a person feel good? I have lost touch with
God! I want Him back. Help me! I am
                        Yours truly,
                        Katharine Johnson

P.S. Did anyone clean out Father Steele's house?
P.S.S. Don't, please, contact me in person, but by mail.

Stretched on the floor, beside the fire, Lachlan and Caralisa smoked and drank wine. It was only ten, but he felt he should leave soon, before he could give himself away. He couldn't take his eyes off her! Pink lips, black eyelashes, smooth wrists and long skinny legs, and all her gestures, quick and nervous, suffused his cheeks with a hot glow.

Religious discussions had long since flown. His pomposity had dissolved over dinner. She was talking, now, about how marriage can ruin a good friendship. He watched her lips, but hardly heard a word she said. Her dark and exotic beauty, he realized, again, would never bore him. But then he had never had sex with someone who looked foreign, almost revolutionary! This thought made him sit upright. He considered it bad taste to think such things, after all. Even Mother would find her beautiful, he told himself.

"What's wrong?" she asked.
    "Nothing, why?"
"You looked like you heard something."
    "No, no," laughing.
"It gets lonely out here in the woods."
    "It must. Do you get scared, alone?"
"No. I mean, I have David."
    "A child could hardly protect you."
"It gives me a feeling of protection," she said, "even if it's irrational."
    "I understand."
"But sometimes I wake up too early, before the sun is up, and lie there, hearing noises."
    "Animals."
"Skunks, raccoons, but still, it gives me the creeps."
    "Can you go back to sleep?"
"No! I wait for the sun. I worship the sun," she said, "coming from a sunny climate, like I do. Sometimes I go and get in bed with David."

"What would Freud say about that?"
"Well, David is asleep, he doesn't even know I'm there."
"It sounds very — sad," he said.
"No, no, it isn't," eager to prove her strength.
"I hate to leave you alone here."
"You're going?"
"I better. It's late."

She sprang to her feet first. Dejection crawled into her, she tried a smile. He reached up a hand, she took it, and pulled him to his feet.
"I'm getting old," he said.
"You don't look it."

Holding onto her hand, he looked down to her and asked if he could come back the following night.
"After dinner?"
"For dinner, if you want."
"I have to eat with some boring people. Then I can come," he said.
"Fine."
He kissed the palm of her hand, released it and walked to get his coat. Her grief was so great, watching him depart, that then, alone, she crept into David's bed, without even trying her own.

In the town library there was an atmosphere Kathy had come to prefer more than the church she no longer attended. The two elderly women who ran the place spoke in soft voices. Two armchairs faced racks of magazines; there was a large section in the rear of the building, sunny and lined with children's books and small chairs. Downstairs, dark and warm, were the stacks, where Kathy would sit on the floor, reading.

Her original purpose for coming there — to uncover the history of the Rectory, its GHOST — was quickly abandoned. She perused old books, instead, photographs of cities, boats, dams, railroads, people. The geography section held her attention for several days after school, then fiction, which she had never liked before, for its being false, grabbed her. *The Purloined Letter* by Poe was a great discovery; the word *purloin* excited her before she knew what it meant.

Pearl, loin, pearly loins, purloin like a neon fish, darting in green aquarium reeds — what a word! Then to discover it meant 'to steal, pilfer, take dishonestly' struck her as a form of revelation. She had been attracted to the word, consciously ignorant of its meaning, but maybe subconsciously aware of its special meaning for her. And it occurred to her that words were magic in some way, that fiction was true, not false, that she was on the track of Truth!

She read, voraciously, till late into the night. The homework she got could be accomplished in a half hour. Then, at last, she was free to lie in bed with a book or to squat between the stacks in the library, inhaling the dense, fertile smell of old print.

The Church, now, in contrast, appeared forbidding, cold, glacial. She was scared to return there. When she left the library, at closing time, in the dark, the bells were playing their six o'clock hymn from across the Green — a sound that filled her with dread, for all the memories it recalled.

Dear Father St. George,
     This is just a note to ask if you can help me. I feel like a
walnut!
               There was a little green house
               And in the little green house
               There was a little brown house
               And in the little brown house
               There was a little yellow house
               And in the little yellow house
               There was a little white house
               And in the little white house,
               There was a little heart.
That's me. How does a person feel good? I have lost touch
with God! I want Him Back. Help me! I am
                         Yours truly

                         Katharine Johnson
     P.S. Did anyone clean out Father Steele's house?
     P.S.S. Don't, please, contact me in person, but by mail.

Lachlan stared at her handwriting, which was round and childish, to his surprise. He would have expected a more conven-
tional high school cursive curl. Yet he remembered having an
inkling of her mental derangement, a sense that she wasn't
altogether what she seemed to be. He was embarrassed for her,
in a way; but he liked being called upon for help.

His failure with the parents had convinced him that he must not
stay in Ashville. His mother was pulling strings in Boston. His
only purpose, now, in staying was the conquest of Caralisa. He
would write to the Bishop and explain, honestly, his discomfort
at being in suburbia, or exurbia, or the country, or whatever it
was called. He read Kathy's letter over again, and again. Then
he wrote back, at once:

Dear Kathy,

Thank you for writing to me. You describe very vividly your state of mind; it is not an uncommon one. I think you may be suffering from a feeling of guilt, regarding Father Steele. He did not, I understand, have a very happy view of God, and he might have influenced you towards the same point of view. But you must try not to feel responsible for his suicide, or in any way implicated.

I myself have always had a pretty comfortable relationship with our Maker — feeling He is more of a grandfather than a father. That is, He does not confuse himself with me, as a father does, and pass judgement on all my actions. But, on the contrary, He is distant, forgiving and amused even by my failures and weaknesses.

How does a person feel good, you ask. By leading a balanced life, by struggling to improve oneself, and by prayer. If you pray with an uneasy, nervous, guilt-ridden heart, you will be answered by none other than a mirror of your own ego. But if you pray with an open and loving heart, I can say, with conviction, that you will be answered by an open and loving heart.

I would like to be able to talk to you, face to face, in greater depth; but if this is difficult for you, you can write me again or meet me in the confessional on a Saturday afternoon.

P.S. A cleaning company is due to clean up the Rectory in a week. The movers will be coming soon after that.

The bells were ringing when Elmer noticed Kathy. She was passing the drugstore, head down, toting a pile of books. The night was bitter and windy, branches cracking off shields of frost.

Need a lift?
Oh thank you.
Hop up, and in.
She climbed inside and slammed the door. It was like driving in a truck with her father, up so high like that. Music was playing on the radio. The van was all shiny and warm, with a good stiff smell of leather.
How do you like it, he asked.
It's beautiful!
Thanks. I like it myself.
When are you taking off?
A couple of weeks.
He turned down the wide road that led to her family's development. About half a mile, he drove slowly.
Want to go for a ride?
I better not. Homework, and my Mom.
It's just six. I'll have you back at six-thirty.
Her bowels squirmed uneasily. She glanced at his well-cut profile, his internalized and surprised stare.
I don't think I better, she said.
No one seems to want to ride with me, he said.
The complaint in his voice was real enough, she responded to it warmly, but let the weight of the books on her lap sink deeper, reassuringly.
Okay. I'll go for a ride, she said.
Just a quick one.
He relaxed his shoulders and smiled, speeding up as they passed her place and headed towards the less populated area of town. No streetlights, he turned his beams on bright. She began to enjoy it quickly, the passage away, branches like loose wires, a few bright stars. He asked her if she saw the eclipse the other

night, she said no, she was in the library and missed it, he said it
was pretty interesting, a total eclipse, doesn't happen too often,
she must like to read alot to miss something like that. I have a
term paper, she said, and the best place to work is the library.
Boy, it feels good to get out of town for a few minutes, like this, I
can see why you're taking off. I'll be glad to leave, he said, real
glad.

 Someday I'll leave too.

 Head south, you said, I remember.

 But I want to have a purpose when I go, she said.

 Like what.

 Like a job, or a school, something.

 Not me, I just go for the sake of going.

 You must feel at home in the world.

 Maybe not.

 I don't.

 Why not?

 Who knows?

 Graduation jitters, maybe.

 Really?

 I've seen it happen.

 Like what?

 They just freak out. Scared to leave home.

 Not me.

 Sure?

 Positive.

 Okay.

She leaned over and turned up the volume on a song she liked,
leaned back and looked out as they swung up onto the highway.
This was the Sea of Tranquility.

 We'll go to the next exit, then turn around, he said.

 It's a good smooth ride.

 Go to sleep.

 Ha.

They smiled to themselves and he turned off at the first exit.

 I'll drive down behind the orchards, he said.

 Okay.

 It's prettier than the highway.

You get sick of highways.

I'm going south by the back roads.

Then what?

I'll stop when I run out of cash. We've got fifteen more minutes till six-thirty.

He slowed down, the road was winding and familiar, nearer to the high school, her books seemed to sleep on her lap like a child as she rocked with the curves. She felt she could go on riding alot longer.

I hate my home, she announced.

He didn't reply, but glanced at her for the first time, then back at the road.

I have a friend who lives back in those woods there, he said, alone with her kid.

Your girlfriend?

It doesn't matter.

Not if you're leaving, I guess.

Right.

As if the air had suddenly heated from this exchange, he unrolled his window a trifle, the cold slipped in like a sword.

I hope, when I'm your age, I'll feel at home in the world, too, said Kathy.

Do I seem alot older to you?

Yes.

Weird. More experienced?

Lots.

I guess you're still a juvenile, legally speaking.

That's right, she said.

You could get away with murder.

They laughed. Then he remembered her getting caught stealing and he held his breath.

Your hair looks better, as I said, he said.

This remark, trivial as it was, contained enough significance to throw them into an embarrassed silence. Elmer began, mentally, to compare Kathy to Caralisa. Kathy was more to his understanding, and therefore liking. Her questingness subverted complacency, a quality he couldn't abide. Caralisa's idealism was a form of complacency, even arrogance, as he saw it. She really believed there was no such thing as error; all events were meant to be, and for the good. Still, she held him in thrall, attached, as if he was related to her, could not back off, just because of minor disapproval. The irrationality of this emotion angered him, and he felt he should, could, break the spell, by some action.

Want to come back to my place? he asked Kathy.

What for, she said.

To sit, talk, etcetera.

No. I want to go home.

You sure know what you want all the time.

He pulled the car to the side of the road, and Kathy's head turned, startled, her eyes luminous.

Don't be scared, he said, I just want to talk. To someone.

He turned off the engine, and leaned on the wheel heavily.

Are you still shop-lifting? he asked her.

How did you know?

Just did.

No. I'm not, she said.

That's good. It's stupid. Anyone can steal, and does. Even rich kids.

I know some that do, said Kathy.

My uncle was an atheist, said Elmer, but he had morals. War. He fought in the War. He was a communist for awhile. Always stayed on that side of things, though he didn't go to meetings.

Kathy listened with some interest. Her freeze of anxiety was dissolved by his posture. She guessed he was lonely.

He read all the papers, helped organize a clinic, and the grape boycott, he got behind that too. He raised me from five years on. I have alot of old buddies from school, now they're in some house of correction. Petty crime. Stupid, Criminals should put their anger to better use. As my uncle said. The jails are full of ignorant revolutionaries. That's what he said.

You miss him?

No. He talked to himself when he was talking to me. But he gave me some ideas. Like how obeying the law is really a

way of staying free. They define you, once you've com-
mitted a crime. You're labelled. You're not free anymore.
That's why I obey the law.
Always?
    Well, almost always.
What happened to your parents?
    I don't have a father. My mother died when I was small.
What of?
    Stupid. She choked. On food. Peanut butter. Be careful if
    you ever eat peanut butter. A big bite of it can kill you.
He leaned back then, and Kathy automatically tilted towards
the door. But he started the engine.
    You're scared of me, I can tell, he said, I'll take you on
    home. But it might be fun to go for a longer drive sometime
    before I leave.
Where to?
    Maybe Providence.
I wish I could go all the way.
    What?
I mean all the way south – far. You know.
    Ha, I didn't think you meant what I heard.

SIX

*

What attracted men to Caralisa – and she knew this – was the exact quality which caused her to lose them. Childlike, childish, they merged and became the same, in time, in her. It was not an act; it was character, her own. She had moments, and now was one of them, when she believed she could turn into someone else. Mature in a matter of seconds, like a Disney flower unfolding on screen.

Hope was the exotic nutrient which brought on these unexpected blooms. Hope of being saved, consoled, and held secure without sacrifice. She had had no such hope with Elmer, though he certainly offered it to her, freely. She had such hope with Lachlan, and it made her feel the way she suspected everyone else in the world always feels. Powerful. Centered. On target. Righteous.

So she sat down and wrote to Bob: "I have custody of David, and I plan to keep it that way." It was one of the few letters in her life she would actually mail.

*

I hate myself for feeling this way, said Elmer.
Don't, replied Caralisa, It's only natural.
You're seeing that minister again.
Yes, she admitted easily.
So I guess that means you'll be staying here. Not coming
with me.
I guess so. But I never actually said —
I know you didn't.
I mean, I really like you and all —
Don't say that.
You can come see me before you go, okay?
Right, said Elmer and rang off, I can.

When she hung up the phone, it was nearly noon. Shudders of
pleasure passed through her, as she headed downtown to pick
David up from school. It was a dank cold day, snow was imminent in the yellowing rims on clouds, she always wondered how
birds kept warm and where they went on days like these. They
all up and disappeared. Clumps of brown grass along the
riverbed were glued together by white ice. In town the greens for
Christmas had been strung up over the shop windows and the
doors of the two churches. Red bows and silver glitter in the
windows. She decided she would treat herself to a new blouse
and take David with her, shopping.

*

It was all unexpected, but in the voluminous department store she was hit with a gust of emotion — anxiety or longing, it was hard to pin a term on it — and she leaned against a counter full of skirts for support. David was in the toy department, examining cars, but it felt as if he were miles away from her or as in dreams she used to have, shortly after his birth, it was as if he was drowning in a black sea, already invisible underwater, when she arrived to save him, totally hidden, no way to part the waves to find and save him. She stood staring at the tinsel dripping from the high ceiling, then moved her eyes, stealthily, along racks of dark men's jackets, to a heap of Christmas wrapping paper and ribbons.

David! she shouted.
No one thought it strange to have her there, shouting, for there was no one there. The store appeared abandoned by humans, left in a hurry, all the goods cast down in flight.
David!
He shouted back.
What?
Are you all right?
Come see this truck!
Coming!
She lurched forward, trailing his voice, he was still yelling out details about the truck, like crumbs, Hansel's mechanics in the huge forest, she followed, before they were swept away, his words, and found him crouched on the floor with a huge yellow truck.
How much does it cost? she asked.
He looked all over for a tag, but she found it first, kneeling on the floor beside him.
Fifteen dollars. God.
For Christmas?
She looked it over, it was made of strong steel, not plastic, she tugged at the wheels to see if they sat tight.
Ah, I'll get it now, she said.

Really, Mom? Really?
Yeah, come on, let's go.
I'll show it to Elmer.
Why would you want to do that?
He'd like it.
Why do you like him so much?
I don't know.
She found a check-out line by the sound of one voice and a bell, and went there, trailing David, figuring she didn't need a blouse anyway. But her brain was racing, she didn't dare turn around to look back into the tinsel-filled barn, though the vision hung onto her back like a touch of madness, lost love. She just wanted to get out of the store. David's bliss was buoyant and catching, it held her up till she was out in the grey day again. She took a deep breath.

Inside the car together, warm, she sat with him looking at the bright yellow truck.
I'm glad you like it, she told him.
Can I show it to Elmer?
Sometime, I guess.
I like him, David said after a pause, because he's normal.
Normal?
He just does things. You know. Stupid Lachlan talks all the time.
That's because he's intelligent.
Well, I like Elmer because he does things, David said, contented with his own judgement.
His small and dirty hand was caressing the hood of the truck, when Caralisa grabbed it and planted a kiss on its palm.

*

Elmer took his place beside the window, where a moon-like sickle of ice glazed the glass. He breathed on it, melting a space for his eyes to peer through. It was much the same scene as before— the minister was sitting at the table, with wine, smoking, and Caralisa was poking at food in the oven. David was on the floor with a big yellow truck, packed with blocks, moving along on his knees, in his flannel pajamas. A fire. All the accoutrements of home and hearth and happiness.

Slight snowdrops began to emerge. No stars through the muffler of clouds overhead. The weatherman had predicted an inch of snow tonight, turning to sleet by morning. Elmer had no precise sense of humiliation, this time, in his position; indeed, he felt nothing at all. He could hear music playing in the house, soft stuff, classical, without words, but it failed to move him. Music was, generally, the source of emotion for Elmer, the whole source; when there was no radio playing, he was hardly aware of his own presence on earth. He might be working on a car, with a machine, and the music in the service room was cut off from his hearing, and then he would just be doing the job, one machine approaching another. When the machine stopped, the sparks settled around his feet, and the disk jockey's voice trailed off into music, he was stirred awake, played upon himself, as an instrument.

He stood stock still, numb to the core, observing the scene inside. Caralisa said something to the minister, who got up and went to the oven, where he began stirring the contents of a pot with a wooden spoon, while Caralisa took David to bed. There was some conversation; David, reluctantly, went to the minister and let him kiss his cheek goodnight. Then the boy scooped up his truck and carried it, awkwardly, to his room. Left alone in the kitchen, the minister stirred slowly and absent-mindedly, an expression of pleasure on his curling lips. Caralisa returned quickly and took her place beside him; they looked into the pot, then each took a taste of the yellowish sauce off the tip of the wooden spoon.

Elmer looked at his dark sleeve, where flakes of snow were settling. Then he blew on the window pane and peered in. He saw the minister turn the flame off under the pot, and as Caralisa began to move, reach for her and turn her against him. They kissed, on the mouth, she had to strain upwards, being much smaller, the minister's hand was on the small of her back.

Elmer took a jacknife out of his pocket. It was heavy. He walked down along the side of the house to the front, where the two cars—hers and his—were parked side by side. A film of snow was gathering on the cold steel. He leaned down behind Lachlan's car and made a small gash, with the heavier blade, through the thick rubber beside the hub cap. Then he walked on up the quiet road to his own van, and drove home.

*

Lachlan had driven over slowly that night. He was commanding himself to slow down in all directions. Not to leap into bed with Caralisa was the first instruction; not to tell her of his plans for them was the second; and not to grab any job in Boston was the third. Patience! Caution!

He was still absolutely convinced that she was the woman sent by the Grace of God to share his life with him. And he had an almost superstitious sense that he shouldn't sleep with her before they were married, or it would be ruined. Something would go wrong between them. The whole structure of their affair must be different from those he had before.

His main fear was that he would spill the beans and start talking, impetuously, to her. He would tell her everything that was on his mind. His tongue was beyond his control. Language was not only the chief means of his support, his profession,but was that direct result of all that he observed or felt. He loved to talk!

Well, he was allowed to kiss her, finally; he let himself do that much, in the kitchen, and, overwhelmed with emotion, had to sit down immediately afterwards. His instant defense was speech.

> You never know another person completely, he babbled. They are always eluding you. Just as you are always being eluded, internally, by your own sense of self, you can never be sure who another person is.

I know what you mean, she replied, but I think it's worse between men and women than between women and women. And I think I know my child pretty well — as well as I know myself.

> Maybe, he said, but he might surprise you yet.

Don't say that. It scares me.

They ate boiled salmon steaks with herb sauce, broccoli and Italian bread. A half-gallon of white chablis stood between them. He had bought the salmon steaks and the wine. They had both agreed they preferred fish to meat.

She gobbled down her food, he was leisurely, or so filled with strong feeling, he could hardly swallow. Grief, pity, longing, love, he tried to identify each wave of emotion as it swelled down his arms and legs and throat. He started to talk about God as the most elusive being of all, as being everywhere visible and invisible at the same time.

She tried to listen, but the subject of God made her uneasy. It made her think of shoulds and should-nots, the great oppressive city at the top of her head. As soon as he mentioned God, she was reminded of his extraordinary profession. Even if he chewed with his mouth open, stretched and belched, his breath was tinted with incense, lilies grew on his chest. She must be upright, while her organs clapped like castanets at the thought of his kiss.

Ah, that was wonderful, he sighed, expanding, and smiled warmly at her.
Do you want some cheese, coffee?
No, let's sit in front of the fire. It needs another log.
They're all outside, in the basement.
I'll get them, he said.
She cleared the table while he got his jacket.
Oven flowers, he said, that's what some poet—I can't remember who—called the pink that comes to a woman's cheeks after cooking. You've got them.
He put his hands on her warm cheeks, kissed her, and then went out. He was elated to discover it was snowing and stood, hands in pockets, watching it swing, like chains of beads, in the faint chill wind. His eyes travelled over the tops of the trees, he said an involuntary prayer of gratitude, and was about to start for the basement, when he noticed the odd tilt of his car. He headed down to it, directly, and discovered the flat tire. Oh crap, he said, and gave the car a kick.

*

"I've got a flat tire," he announced.
He dropped four logs in front of the hearth.
"Oh no," she cried, "Do you have a spare?"
"I do, thank God."
"Do you want to change it now or later?"
"I'll get it over with."
"I'll come with you."
"No, you stay here. It's snowing out."

She did the dishes then, while he did the car. Something always
goes wrong, she whined inwardly, sighing. She quickly poured
herself and him another glass of wine and laid out the logs on
the bright coals. She was shivering. He would, she was sure, be
so upset by the flat tire, he would leave right away. It would
make him conscious of the dangers in their relationship. After
all, she was a nobody on Welfare out in the woods with a child.
A pre-Christian hedonist, living a blighted forest life. She could
view herself this way, in relation to him, as being on the side of
magic, witches, occult visions, all the accoutrements of a spirit
in firm opposition to the Church.

He, on the other hand, was socially respectable. A bastion of
brahmin ideology! If his car broke down completely outside her
shack, he would be stoned by the public. Or his congregation of
assholes would come in the night with torches and burn her
shack to the ground. She stared at the fire with her eyes burning.
If only she had a job! Something to justify her existence in
society! Anyone can have a baby, raise a child, but mothering
was no longer an excuse for existence. Once, she imagined, it
was sufficient to be a mother, and she would have been pro-
tected by this fact. But now! The fact that you could choose to
be a mother or not, both before and after childbirth, meant that
you couldn't lay back and feel sorry for yourself. She crouched
by the fire, and rocked there, with her hands out, waiting.

He came in with snow in his hair.
"I'm terrible at changing tires," he said, "but I think it will hold till tomorrow."
"But you better drive slowly," rising.
"It looks like there's going to be alot of snow."
"They say only an inch."
"Well I better not stay too long anyway."
"No," squatting.

He threw off his jacket and sat beside her. She moved up and away to sit alone on the couch with a cigarette.
"Where are you going?" he asked.
"I was getting too hot."
Following her, "I hate leaving you alone out here, I really do. It's so isolated!"
"I'm okay."
He sat down beside her, his cheeks were red, his eyes watery, he put his arm around her roughly.
"I love you," he said.
She pressed her face into his neck, eyes wide open, ears pricked.
"You hardly know me," she whispered.
"Yes I do."
She leaned to check his features, but he clamped his hand on her face and kissed her. He had forgotten all his own instructions. His bones were turning out sap. Laying her back, he drove himself against her, she twisted her legs around him. They looked at each other.
"We better wait," she said.
"For what, wait."
"Time."
Kissing her, "You're right."
She pushed him up, then pulled him down, then pushed him up again, wrestling with indecision. Finally, he sat up.
"You're right," he said again.
She slipped her hand between his legs, then pulled it out again, which made him grab for her; but she extricated herself, quickly. She leaned over and tossed her burned-out cigarette square into the fire.
Beamed at him, "I can hardly wait. But will."

*

Elmer dreamed of irreversibles—lost keys, missed connections, late arrivals, too late. He woke up tossing around five and couldn't go back to sleep. These were negative miracles, as powerful as any of the good ones usually sited. They were the miracles of impotence, rejection, error. It was hard to believe; it was wonderful in the oldest sense of the word. He had failed, been rejected, made a mistake.

What had he done wrong in real life? Slept with a woman who cared nothing for him; blown most of his money on an unnecessary van. He had invested time in a plan, an illusion. He had mortified himself as a Peeping Tom. Cut the tire of an older man as if it were a gesture of strength. Pathetic.

What can I do to get over it, he wrestled, stomping around his room in stocking feet. What can I do to forget it? I have to do something to make things right.

*

Elmer had some road calls in the morning, driving the pick-up around town and out to the freeway a few times. He was glad to move around, since he could hardly stand still. Restless as a schizophrenic, he fairly danced while he worked in the afternoon. It was a long wet day, the snow of the night before was rinsed away in morning showers, rows of drops hung off the branches, a white sky.

But around four, when the darkening of the air was just beginning, Lachlan drove into the station. He walked right into the shop where Elmer was doing a tune-up on a Chevrolet Vega.

"Hi there," said Lachlan.

Elmer nodded, wiping grease off his fingers.

"Could you fill her up? And I need a new tire, just a spare, I
      hope, while you're at it."

Elmer looked down, walking out to the pumps. Lachlan opened his trunk and removed the slashed tire, rolling it over to Elmer who stared at the numbers on the pump.

"It's ruined," said Lachlan, "Don't know how or why, but
      it was old anyway. How much is a new one?"

"About thirty bucks."

"Okay."

Elmer glanced at the slashed tire, and at Lachlan—a good- looking dude, he had to admit; but a grimace kept paining his eyes and he had to turn away. Tempted to ask after Caralisa, to ask how's the whore in the woods or did she keep you up all night, to indicate his knowledge of the entire situation, to have an effect—he clammed up.

"Actually," said Lachlan, "I'm not very good at changing
      tires. Would you mind taking a look at the one I put on, just
      to make sure?"

Elmer screwed the cap on the gas tank, then leaned down, quickly over the new tire.

"Something must be wrong," affably, "if you knew right
      away which tire it was."

Elmer flushed, burning, a sudden tension in his upper chest. He didn't reply but removed the hub cap and tested the screws one by one. "The hub was loose," he muttered, replacing it with a hard kick.

"That's all?"
Elmer shrugged, wiped his hands red from cold and stained brown, on his pants, and slouched off to the shop to find a new tire for Lachlan. Lachlan followed him, thinking him very surly and bad-tempered.
"You better pick your tire up in the morning," said Elmer, "I don't have time to get it together now."
The darkness in the sky was increasing by leaps and bounds. Lachlan handed him a ten dollar bill. He watched Elmer ring it up and produce the change, and wondered why he was so insolent.
"Are you alone here?"
"The boss is out on a road call."
"Ah."
"So you better stay close to home tonight," said Elmer.
"Why's that?"
"Without a spare, you never know."
"Oh. Of course. You're right."
Lachlan thanked Elmer, automatically, in a pleasant voice, as soon as he had his change. Elmer stood, with his slashed tire, watching him drive off, with a defeated look.

*

"What are you doing Friday night?" asked Elmer.

"I'm going to Boston!" said Caralisa into the phone.

"Boston."

"To visit some friends."

"I'll be leaving here soon."

"That's too bad."

"I want to see you before I go."

"I could stop by the station."

"No, that's no good."

"Well, then, I don't know when."

"What about tonight?"

Caralisa raked her brain quickly for an excuse. Lachlan couldn't come, he had a meeting, but the last thing she wanted was a visit from Elmer.

"I don't feel too great."

"I won't stay long."

"Okay, after supper, but just for a short time."

"After supper?"

"I don't have any food in the house."

"I could bring some out. A pizza."

"Oh, okay," she sighed. "See you, Elmer."

Whenever people called him by his name, he was suspicious. In the past it meant trouble.

*

I got one with mushrooms and one plain, said Elmer.
Thanks, she murmured.
    David likes his plain, right?
Right.
David was also glad to see Elmer and burrowed into him, before
slipping back to the television. He ate his pizza there, while
Elmer and Caralisa sat at the table. Elmer thought she looked
like the cat who swallowed the mouse. A swollen expression of
happiness on her smooth dark face. Or like the classic version of
the pregnant woman. A heaviness, which slowed down her ges-
tures, usually so quick and nervous; she smiled alot. She was
being very quiet and polite, as one who holds power is apt to be.
So what's been happening? she asked him.
    Nothing much. Getting ready to go.
It seems like yesterday, we just met.
    Not really. Got some wine?
You want some?
    Just a glass.
Never saw you drink before.
He shrugged, ripping at the pizza with his hands and teeth. His
hunger seemed to have no end tonight, but he heard David
yawn.
    Time for David to go to bed, he said.
You're right.
She placed a glass of wine in front of him and went through a
struggle with her son, who didn't want to sleep. He kicked and
tossed against her, half-laughing and half-crying. She had to
smack his butt to get him to go into his room. Then she went
into the bedroom and stayed there, whispering to him for a long
time.

Elmer sipped the wine. It went right to his head. Even a beer
could knock him off balance. If he drank the whole glass of
wine, he knew he would be drunk. He took it slowly, between
large hunks of pizza, waiting for her to come back, his eyes fixed
on a basket of dirty clothes she kept in a corner by the oven.
Hers and David's. He recognized some of her things, the sleeve

of a blouse, some blue corduroy pants, the red nylon panties she had worn.

He sipped more wine, heard her start to leave David, then the boy cry out for her to stay; and she did, sinking down on the bed beside him again; and he remembered her letting him cry other times.

You want more pizza? he shouted.
No, you eat it, she called back.
Shall I put him to sleep?
No, it's okay.
He crammed in another triangle of pizza, unfilled still, and feeling hot, he stood up.
I'll put him to sleep, he said at the bedroom door.
Caralisa's head jerked up, her eyes wary.
Go on, he told her, I'll do it.
She slipped past him and out. He sat beside David and looked at his face, which was streaked with tomato.
Get a washcloth, he shouted, and bring it here.

Caralisa rushed to do as she was told. Then she left the bedroom while Elmer wiped David's face clean and talked to him.
I don't know if I'll see you again. I'm leaving. And you probably will be, too.
Where are you going, asked David.
South
That's down, right?
Right. Down south. Up north.
David looked at the ceiling, and Elmer stood up, pulling the covers up to the boy's neck.
Go to sleep, he said. He had a moment's impulse to warn David of his mother's ability to betray him, them; but the non-speaker in him prevailed, and he left the room in silence.

Caralisa was washing at the sink. Elmer returned to his wine and pizza, but did not sit down to eat.
You never saw my van, he said, but I'm driving down to Providence. With a girl I met. A trial run. It rides real

smooth. She's real pretty, much younger than you.
What does she look like, Caralisa asked.
  Kind of like Ann-Margret.
Oh!
  Yeah, she's cute.
You're still going to leave?
No woman ever stopped me before.

Caralisa glanced at him and saw he had that wolfy look that she
didn't like. His eyes were intense and red.
  Did the Minister help you make up your mind?
About David? Oh yes. I'll hold onto him.
  So how did he persuade you?
Well, just, he told me, you know, to be patient.
  That's not easy for you. Patient.
No.
She snapped a laugh, blushing. Her breathing got high, a little
panicky.
I better check David, she said.
  He's okay.
Well, just to see.
  He's quiet!
Okay. Okay.
Elmer stepped over beside her, at the sink, and watched her
hands moving through pale bubbles. He sensed her recoil.
  I guess I better go, he said.
I don't feel too great. As I mentioned.
  Right.
Her hands lifted out of the water, he watched them slide to a
paper towel, she dried them. Familiar hands, he felt sorry for.
  Don't worry, he said and moved for his jacket.
He knew he could break her in half. But what was the point, he
wondered, in that? Still unsettled, but tempered by the wine, he
went to her door.
  I guess you'll be hearing from me, some day, he said.
I hope so!
The relief in her face was more than he could bear. He didn't
even say goodbye.

*

Till deep into the night Elmer was plagued by the thought of his failure, caused, this time, by pity. He should, at least, have lectured Caralisa on promiscuity and morality. But the limp control she had over her own nest had gotten under his skin, weakening him.

So let her have a ball with the minister, and be happy. So what? he kept repeating. I would've bought a new car soon anyway.

But when Lachlan came to pick up his tire the next morning, Elmer couldn't take his body out from under a car; he didn't want to see the man. He overheard, instead, a jaunty conversation between Sam and Lachlan about weather and unemployment, which made his blood boil.

The difference between one man's destiny and another's struck him as more than an accident of fate, of birth. It was the result of centuries of planning on the part of the rich. To protect their own. Lachlan exuded privilege and self-assurance, the luxury of liberalism. How blandly and pityingly he spoke of the unemployment problem!

As Elmer stared into the dark assemblage of pipes close to his face, he envisioned himself soon, once again, trucking across the surface of the nation, never penetrating those secrets behind the yellow squares of windows at night, children running home from school, men shouting about budgets in city halls, the family circle around a fat turkey. He saw himself burning a circumference, belting through strips of look-alike malls, cheap department stores, till his new van ran out and he had to buy another. What effect would he have before D–TH? Why should he let men like Lachlan enter and control those comforts, while he repeated his family history?

*

At the end of the day, he stood up.

"I'm leaving on Sunday," he told Sam.

"We'll miss you—a great worker."

"Thanks, man."

Sam put twenty bucks, a small bonus, in Elmer's hand. It was Friday and he got his last pay check too. Elmer stuffed his money away and raised his hand, so long.

"Now what did I say I'll do," he asked himself.

Since he always did what he said he would do, his main concern was tying up the loose ends.

"I said I'd take that kid, Kathy, to Providence."

It was dark already, but the Christmas decorations were lit up in the center of town. Elmer stepped in a phone booth and asked Kathy if he could come right over and get her. She sounded surprised, pleased.

"See you," he said.

He wanted to shake up all remnants of grief. For a few minutes, he sat in the van listening to music. While he tried, now, to blame his emotions on the cold climate, the cold people, he was, he realized, getting older. Saying goodbye was getting harder to do. Even if it was just goodbye to a place.

"Sucker," he called himself.

SEVEN

*

The drive down to Providence took about forty minutes. Elmer followed a smooth black highway, nearly deserted, south, country hills on all sides. Signs flared up, indicating life in the black underbrush, human life, though there were no other signs of it. Darkness. Elmer kept the radio tuned to a Hartford station, which had good rock and soul music, few interruptions. He and Kathy hardly spoke for a time, but meditated, separately, out the windows. No presence lounged between them now.

Your mom's a good looking woman, Elmer finally said.

She really is, Kathy agreed.

Creep she's married to.

Wow, that's for sure.

Your dad a creep like that too?

No, but he was a little crazy.

Must be, to leave a pretty lady like that.

Well, you know, he met somebody else.

Probably he regrets it.

Kathy shrugged without conviction. She was feeling nervous already and didn't want to talk too much. She felt swallowed up, like she had nothing to say anyway, and would rather be left alone with her thoughts. It was okay to be on the go, driving, and she had nothing against Elmer, but she wished, now, she had taken a gulp of creme de menthe or coffee brandy before she left the house. No part of her was high.

Elmer let the conversation fizzle. He was thinking of the money in his pocket. He always carried a hundred dollars in cash. The rest he had withdrawn from the bank and was stashed, now, under his mattress, for his trip. He was wondering how far it would carry him, how long, before he would have to get another job in a service station somewhere around Florida. It was good to think about numbers and miles. And he was pleased Kathy was not a big talker, or small talker, but quiet like that.

Providence was like a ghost city. Few lights, few people. They entered over a bridge, crossing a large throughway, there was industry, billboards, the usual hotel turrets, but then, descending into the city itself, all feeling of surprise and function vanished, it looked dingy, a few Christmas lights strung around. They cruised through the streets, looking for an Italian restaur-,ant.

After we eat, we can take in a show, said Elmer.

What's playing?

I dunno, we can get a paper.

They found a restaurant and she followed him in. The place was lit with orange lights, wore checkered tablecloths; the booths along its walls each had a jukebox; and only a handful of people were eating there. Elmer went to a booth and Kathy sat across from him. He flipped for songs to play right off, spilling quarters onto the table, while Kathy stared at the menu.

Eat whatever you want, he said, I'm rich.

Thanks.

I'm going to have veal parmigiana, if they have it.

She looked for it on the menu and found it.

They do, she said.

So what'll you have?

Uh, just minestrone, salad. That's all.

The waitress took their orders, they both drank Coke.

Let's move closer to the speaker, said Elmer, We can't hear the music.

So they switched booths and moved down to the far wall. Kathy was relieved to find herself next to the Ladies Room, and squeezed in her blue jeans pocket the crucifix Frieda gave her. Her face was pale, her eyes brighter than usual. Elmer glanced at her, drumming his fingers in time to the music.

You okay? he asked.

Sure. Fine.

You look kind of tense.

No, I'm not.

Still sing in the choir?

Uh, no.

Why not?

Too much work.

Oh yeah, you're bookish, I forgot.

Not really.

What about that minister?

Which? What about him?

Is he a big influence on you?

I don't go to church any more.

She gazed over his shoulder.

He's not worthy of your attention anyway.

Well, I didn't go to Church to worship him! I used to go because of the other guy, but you know what he did.

Blew his brains out.

Their eyes met, magnetic and blind.

I wish he hadn't, said Kathy.

He probably thought he was doing people a favor.

Really?

Sure, he probably thought he was more trouble than he was worth.

Kathy's eyes lightened, questioning.

When that happens, said Elmer, everything comes out wrong. I mean, when you become too important to yourself. That's my impression.

That's interesting. Really. The new minister said—

I don't want to hear what he said.

Elmer's eyes darkened.

What's so bad about him, asked Kathy.

It's personal. Here's our food.

Elmer sprinkled Parmesan cheese on Kathy's soup and buttered some bread for her, while she watched his hands thoughtfully.

You shouldn't hint at things you're not going to tell, she said.

Let's not ruin a good time, okay?

This instruction touched her, and she put the thought of Lachlan aside. They listened to music while they ate, and he gave her some change to pick tunes on the box. Then he went to the cash register and asked the waitress what shows were playing in town. She got a newspaper out of the kitchen and spread it on the table for him. Kathy watched Elmer from afar, with curiosity. His actions appeared more automatic than those of the usual person, but she couldn't figure out what motivated him.

There's a movie called *Night Moves,* he said, starring Gene Hackman. We can walk there.

He handed her her coat and threw down a dollar tip.

They haven't played all my songs yet, she said.

That's okay, we can always come back and play them again.

I wish—oh well.

What.

She didn't tell him the truth—that she wished he wouldn't leave Ashville until she had figured him out—but said, instead, in self-defense.

I wish you'd tell me about that minister, I really do.

Let sleeping dogs lie, he smiled.

*

Lachlan was wearing his black suit and white collar when he came to get Caralisa on Friday.

I'm running a little late, he said.

What happened?

A funeral.

The collar nearly knocked the breath out of her. It turned him into the walking Image of righteousness!

Your outfit makes me nervous, she confessed.

Oh that's natural, believe me.

Will I get used to it?

Of course.

Are you sure?

You might even find it sexy some day.

They piled into his car for the drive to Boston. David was settled into the back seat with a paper bag on his knees. Lachlan pulled Caralisa right up beside him.

Sit close to me.

He placed her hand between his legs. She turned to look back at David who was seated on the edge of his seat, staring out the window with a petrified expression.

Are you all right, darling? she asked him.

Why are we going to Boston, he said in a flat voice.

I told you.

But why?

To meet Lachlan's family.

Why?

Try to sleep, okay?

Can I have my gum now?

Sure, go ahead.

Sometimes David got car sick, but it was unpredictable. Sometimes he would just go to sleep. As they headed out on the highway, it seemed possible he would sleep this time. Anxiously she kept turning back to look at him. His presence was really ruining everything. She would have far rather met Lachlan's family alone, but there was no way she could leave him behind.

Does your mother like children? she asked.

I don't really know.

I'm sure she'll hate me.

No, she won't. Besides, if we tell her we plan to move to Boston, she'll be happy.

But it's all so sudden!

Don't worry.

And your brother?

Oh, you'll like him.

But what will he think about me?

He'll adore you.

But where will I sleep?

Probably in the guest room, with David.

There are two beds?

Yes. Touch me.

She unzipped his fly.

Will there be a babysitter?

Yes, that's all arranged.

So we can go out tonight?

With Tom. That's right.

We'll crash.

No, we won't.

This is insane.

Tomorrow night we'll be alone again.

Thank God.

She pulled her hand away.

I have to wait twenty four hours? he smiled.

That's right.

She turned, hearing soft choking sounds in the back seat. David had his head in the bag, his shoulders hunched up; he was trying to be quiet about it.

By some quirk of fate, the movie, *Night Moves*, involved a strange search for origins on the part of its hero, a betraying woman, and, strangest of all, Florida's watery landscape. Elmer bit his nails non-stop, disturbed. It was as if he had entered a map of his life, past, present, future. He had flown in, as in a dream, part bird, part aviator, to the land he was aiming for. His temple began to palpitate, the beginning of a full-blown headache, as the movie babbled brightly along; he glanced at Kathy, who sat like a statue, her face holding that glittering immobility she had acquired since cutting her hair. He tried to forget what was going on on the screen and concentrate on her. He put his arm around her and she leaned, somewhat stiffly, against him. He tried to withdraw her attention from the screen to himself, but couldn't. The screen was full of blood and water, and he expected her to cover her eyes, but she didn't. She stared right at it, more than he could manage. Horrible gore! Too much for someone that young, he thought, all the sex and violence. But she wouldn't stop looking and by the end he understood it was he himself who was upset, his head aching, by the way it was about Florida and fucking up and jealousy. What a relief, when the lights went on, and he could start moving away from it. Kathy turned a wide and incredulous face to him. Wow, she said, Gross. I mean beautiful. Incredible! Insane! But he just shrugged saying, it was okay, dully, as his headache spread.

As soon as they entered Boston, Lachlan changed. Caralisa felt estranged, tense. The luminous, langorous, lazy man she had left home with, was now an uptight Minister. Even his accent altered, becoming faintly British and terse. The city, which she had left some years before, hunched up, lighted in the night, and filled her with foreboding. Like a huge devouring animal pretending to be a city, it seemed to breathe by the banks of the river. She had lived, with Bob, in a frenzy. What if she met one of the many men she had screwed then? What if she ran into an old friend from the university? She had not prepared herself for this emotion; in her usual impulsive fashion, she had plunged out with Lachlan to meet his family, forgetting Boston was a place she, too, had lived.
How are you, he asked.
Oh fine, she said.
But her only comfort came from David who needed mothering, attention. She poured over him, carrying the little paper bag full of throw-up with one hand, and holding his hand with the other. They walked to the door of Lachlan's house in silence. He used the key to let them in.

The mother emerged from the gloom, tall as a centurion, a ruined Roman face. She held out her hand and Caralisa had to move the bag of vomit around to shake it. A tight squeeze; David clung to her leg.
    This is Caralisa, said Lachlan beaming.
How was your drive?
    Fine, but I think David needs to wash up.
Show Caralisa the spare bedroom and bathroom then, Dear, said Mrs. St. George.
    Is Tom here?
Oh yes, we're just shaking up the martinis.
    Ah good.
Lachlan led Caralisa and David up some lumpy stairs to the second story, where antiques shuddered on the walls and little tables as they passed. Her room was at the end of the corridor,

and it held two very comfy-looking beds, a television, books, bureaus and photographs. A bathroom adjoined it, and there Caralisa hastened, dragging David behind her.

Wait for me, she called to Lachlan.

I'll be right back, he said, I want to change.

Rubbing David's face and hands, Caralisa thought of her own mother with longing. Oh Juanita, what a kick you'd get out of this whole scene! The sense of history, America's cluttered and eclectic past, even filled the bathroom. Oval bars of yellow soap, monogrammed towels, tiles, a marble sink like a trough, a bathtub with paws for supports. She flushed the bag of vomit down the toilet, but it got stuck, and she had to reach her hand into the icy water to pull it out and dispose of it in an elegant handpainted wastebasket.

Oh shit, she whispered washing her hands.

What do we do now, asked David.

Come downstairs with me. Meet the people.

I don't want to.

Well, you have to.

I'm tired. I want to watch t.v.

Okay, just come down and say hello. Then I'll bring you up here to bed.

But I'll be scared!

I'll sit with you, I promise.

But I'm hungry!

Okay, it's okay, I'll get food.

She brushed his hair in quick flashes, while he winced. She was almost completely out of control, physically, she was so tense. Her elbows, like swords, kept jabbing at objects; she even brushed the side of David's face, so he screamed.

Oh God, God, she said.

Relax, said Lachlan from the door.

She brushed my cheek! cried David.

They all bustled downstairs then, Lachlan in the rear. When they entered the livingroom, Tom and Mrs. St. George stood up to greet them and get them drinks. Caralisa sank into an armchair with David tucked between her legs.

Now what should I get for David, asked the mother.

Anything. A coke?

I thought he might want to go right to bed and watch television, so I asked Lucy to bring him up with a tray. She's the daughter of my housekeeper, and she's very good with children. Is that all right?

Fine, said Caralisa, just fine.

She ignored David's look of wild terror and reached out her hand eagerly for a drink. There was something odd about the mother; she carried a glossy black purse on her arm everywhere she went. It was as if she was on a permanent trip to catch a bus, and afraid of being mugged, at the same time.

Do you want to stay here instead? asked Tom, approaching David and squatting before him. Tom had a sallow, placid face with a receding hairline, boyish good looks gone bad in a man.

David recoiled and shrugged, squeezing his mother's knees.

He loves t.v. she said.

All right, said Tom nasally, I think Star Trek is on now. Shall I bring you up and watch it with you?

Okay, said David.

Tom took his hand and, stooping naturally, led him away.

Relieved as she was, Caralisa suspected a plot. Mrs. St. George undoubtedly wanted to sum her up in private. Or just with Lachlan. And now she missed the weight of her child between her legs, at least a distraction, a justifiable object for her attentions. She stared, rather suspiciously, at the older woman kneading her purse on her knees.

What an amusing little boy, said Mrs. St. George.

He's very good, said Lachlan.

You must be starving. I ordered a roast beef, it's Lachlan's favorite, I hope you like it. She's not the best cook in the world, but she can do Yorkshire pudding quite well.

I do like it, said Caralisa and thanked her stars she never mentioned vegetarianism to Lachlan.

Well now, when do you two plan to be married?

As soon as I've got a new job lined up.

I've heard of a couple of places. I'll talk to you about them
later. Now do you plan to have a church wedding?
Of course!
       But what is the status of Caralisa's first marriage?
She was not married in the church.
       Well then, isn't that good. We should do it here. In your
       father's church.
Fine with me, he said.
       Will your people want to come too? asked Mrs. St. George.
Well, they're way out west, said Caralisa.
       Oh that's too bad.
Not too bad at all, thought Caralisa quickly. Her parents would
look like swine among lambs. She imagined her father in his
shoe-string tie and flowered short sleeve shirt, sitting in this
room, and then her mother bashing out Wagner on the baby
grand piano in the corner. Juanita would love the place, but
make a fool of herself in the process of loving it. Caralisa gulped
her drink, her eyes fixed on Lachlan for help. But he didn't look
back at her. He was lounging on a little love- seat, clumsy and
distracted, and began to talk to his mother about the kind of job
he would like. But Mrs. St. George interrupted him, suddenly,
with a large toothy smile at Caralisa.
       What a beauty you are, she said, So amusing.
These words, like a signal, made Lachlan rise, and he moved
over to sit on the arm of Caralisa's chair, his face flushed with
pleasure. Caralisa understood, then, the source of his tension,
and took his hand.

✳

Roast beef, string beans, potatoes, gravy and Yorkshire pudding, ice cream with chocolate sauce, French wines, candles in silver candlesticks, a white tablecloth, a bowl of yellow roses. The maid came and went, softly, and Mrs. St. George kept her handbag erect on her knees while she ate, and Tom threw out compliments to Caralisa. "Marvelous...a sprite!...She looks fifteen...Pocohantas!"

Let's go out, he concluded, to the Hotel Vendome and get roaring drunk.

Fine with me, said Lachlan, and he eyed, Caralisa noted, his brother with great tenderness. She did too. He radiated benign but total failure in the world, a condition she found reassuring for its familiarity. And she felt he knew her, too, deeply, quickly, as a soulmate.

I'll go check on David, she said and fled, radiant from the table, her suspicions dissolved in alcholol and flattery.

The family listened to her retreating tread, then leaned in towards the center of the table to talk. Their voices were low.

So you really like her, said Lachlan.

I adore her, Tom murmured.

She seems very quiet and pleasant, Mrs. St. George put in, But I'm a bit worried about the problem of the child.

What problem?

Well, to start out a new job, marrying a divorced woman is one thing. But the child will serve as a constant reminder, and won't be good for you at all.

There's nothing to be done. He exists.

There's no way, she suggested, that he could be persuaded to live with his father? She did say the father wants him.

But she wants him too. And she has custody.

Well, I suppose that's that, then, but I do wish it were a somewhat cleaner slate.

To me, it's clean, said Lachlan proudly, I think of her as a virgin in every sense.

Well, she's very amusing, said his mother, Don't you think so, Tom?

Amusing? Very.

The word 'amuse' was one this mother used often. It had a wide range of meanings, including *to entertain, excite to criticism, confirm the worst, comfort*. By her tone of voice, or a shift of lip, you could interpret which meaning she had in mind.

I just don't want you to marry for the sake of marrying, she continued, and this event has a vaguely desperate aura around it.

No, Lachlan protested, it doesn't.

Well, then, I wish you the best. At least it may bring you back to Boston.

She rose from the table and headed, a woman of stiff steps, for the livingroom and brandy. Tom tipped closer to Lachlan, and murmured,

She's right, in her awful way. Better you should bring your vices to the surface than to continue hiding them.

My vices?

Sex, drink smoke—whatever! For years you've been living your life under a huge hood. Separation of church and state, so to speak. Just like poor father, who didn't believe more than in the literary merit of scripture, but pretended he did.

Tom!

Well? It's true. Mother, at least, is an honest atheist.

I'm not an atheist, said Lachlan, whether you like it or not. I've got what's called the gift of faith. I've had it since childhood.

Of course you do, said Tom in a soothing voice, as if Lachlan were still in childhood. But you don't need to be ashamed of your humanity, too.

Well, in this regard you're right, said Lachlan.

So let's get Pocahantas and have a drink—after amusing Mother, of course.

Caralisa sat on the edge of David's bed. The television was rattling along, but David looked petrified, his head sticking out from under the covers. She kissed him.

I'll be sleeping in here, too, she told him.

Now?

No, later.
But why are we here?
I told you. To meet Lachlan's family.
But why?
Because we're getting married.
What about Elmer?
Elmer!
Where is he?
I don't know. Gone.
But I thought we were going with him.
No. Never. I never said that.
Yes you did.
No I didn't. I might have said we might.
Well, why didn't we?
He's going away alone.
But why are we here? I want to go home.
Shut up and go to sleep.
I don't like Lachlan.
You better... Why not?
He smells of smoke.
Well, so do I.
You do not. Not like him.
Well, he's nice. Believe me.
He stinks. I want Daddy.
Shut up.
I want Daddy.
I'll kill you.
I want Daddy.
Okay, you can have him.
Really?
No, I'm joking.
Don't tell jokes!
Go to sleep, David, I'll be up soon.
Kiss me.
Where?
On my tongue.
She kissed his tongue.
I'm scared, he said.

You can leave on the television.
And the light?
No, just the television.
I'm scared of the dark.
The television makes a light.
I want the real light too.
No, shut up!
I'll tell on you.
Tell what?
She went to the door.
About Elmer.
Okay, I'll turn off the t.v.
No!
She turned it off, he shouted.
Are you going to tell? she asked.
NO!
Okay then.
She turned the t.v. on again and left the room. David switched on the light beside his bed and sat up on the pillow.

*

Elmer and Kathy sat in his van outside the Italian restaurant.
     You sure you don't want a coke, he said.
     No, I'm fine, really.
     Okay then, I guess we can start back.
He let the engine idle, warming up, and noted she wore a flat
dreamy expression now, still reflecting the effects of the movie.
His head was full of pain.
     You really liked that movie, didn't you.
     It was wonderful! she said.
     It didn't shock you?
     Which part?
     The sex? the blood?
     No, I've been to movies before, you know.
     And it never shocked you?
     No.
     But what do you know about any of that stuff?
     Never mind, she said.
He was suspicious on the right side of his head, the side she sat
on, and glanced at her fast.
     I thought we were buddies.
     Well, you won't tell me about the minister.
     Nothing, except he's sleeping with the woman I told
you about—lives in the woods with her kid, remember?
     You're kidding.
     No.
     Well, I'd have to see it to believe it.
She looked out the window, eyes blazing.
     They're out of town.
     They can't be. Ha. He has to be at the church tomorrow. So.
     So what? They're out of town tonight then.
They exchanged painful looks.
     But he just got here! said Kathy.
Elmer shrugged, turned down the heat and turned up the music
as they swung back up onto the highway.
     Forget it. It's not important, he said.
     Yes it is. You're telling me the man's a phoney.

Sex doesn't make a man a phoney.

Something about it does, in this case.

Something about it! Like what?

Elmer's voice expressed pleasure in the exchange.

It's hard to explain.

Maybe if you weren't a virgin, you wouldn't be such a tough judge.

Kathy startled him by jerking her head around to land a hard look at him.

Maybe not, she said, but I am.

I could, should, do something about that, he thought, right now, tonight. Seduce her, get it over with. Feel better, more like a man.

Come over here, he said and patted the space beside his right leg.

What for.

Just to be close. So what.

You don't care about me, she said.

He thought this means she's desperate for love. That's what they say when they're ready.

Sure I do. I care alot. Come on.

She moved about two inches.

I'm not really good at flattery, said Elmer, Besides I think we understand each other pretty well without talking.

He put his hand out to her knee. She let it lie there, then moved another two inches closer.

That's better, he said.

And it was. For his head, and his heart. His tensions began to turn off like lights in a prison. She leaned her body against him, while he drove with one hand.

In Elmer's room they stretched on his bed. Kathy had thrashed around like this before, with her mouth and eyes open, 'like a baby bird', said Elmer. She had locked legs, hands, arms, lips, listening, acutely, for words of love. The words made the absurd posture of it all acceptable, turned comedy into tragedy. Elmer was the most silent and the most skilled and the best looking of any boy she had necked with before. His silence was the sticking point.

A couple of phrases, and his lips were sealed. The bed was like a nest, to her, at the top of a tree. There was no room around them, just this suspended vehicle for their actions. She waited, and listened. He got them both stripped, and vanished. She waited and listened, to water and drawers. Afloat, aloft. Unfamiliar smells blew in to her, making distinctions. Not the smell of her own bed, her own house, her mother who was, to Kathy, love incarnate.

When he returned, he pulled back the sheet and climbed inside, seeing her despair.
    Don't let me down, he said.
    But you don't love me.
    I don't love anyone.
    The woman in the woods.
    What's love anyway?
    Mom, said Kathy.
    What?
She didn't answer, so he made a move on her, dying to break her tensions and his own returning. If he didn't, he was sure he would kill someone.
    Don't let me down, he said again, please.
But even though there was something in his tone, which made her pity him, there was nothing in her body to answer that tone.
    I can't, she said.
    Good.
    No, I mean I can't do it.

He lay across her, unmoving, except for his breathing which was short and raw. She didn't move either. Her eyes were shut tight, and her face was screwed up into a knot's closure. She might have been lying on Father Steele's bed again. Dots of her own red blood blazed in her eyelids.

　　You have to. Now, he said, you can't take it back.

　　Please?

　　No.

And he moved again, this time roughly, on top of her. All the struggle he got from her—a sharp knee, a raised hip, pushing hands—came to him as messages of love and desire, and he answered these messages, verbally aloud, until his language made her believe, give up and in, as if it mattered that she was renouncing her source of refuge, and as if he cared.

*

Caralisa spent Saturday morning decorating the Christmas tree with Mrs. St. George and David. Lachlan and Tom had gone out together, somewhere, and Caralisa, poisoned by alchohol and nictotine from the night before, was filled with a humid nausea. Infantile yearnings, vague paranoia. Her only comfort was her son. He was given all the wooden and unbreakable ornaments to hang on the lower branches; it was just the sort of activity which brought out the best in him, a specific task.

"You will come for dinner the day after Christmas, won't you, and bring David?" asked Mrs. St. George.

"Oh I hope so."

"Of course Lachlan has to stay with his parish on Christmas day, but then he'll be free."

"David will, I think, be staying with his father."

"Does he do that often?"

"Every other weekend."

"Ah, but what will happen if you move up here?"

"We'll just have to see."

"Of course."

Mrs. St. George drifted to the window and pulled back the curtain to look out. Her black bag nested under her forearm.

"The snow has already started," she said.

"Snow!" shouted David.

"Yes, it's supposed to go on for days."

"A blizzard?" Caralisa moved to the window. "Oh dear. I hope we get home all right."

She stared at the chains of snowdrops whirling before the facades of brick, the other side of the street, and strained to see if Lachlan was returning. In the corners of her eyes furniture and cloth wobbled to life, dots of activity blown out of her nerves. Smashed until 2 a.m., the surface of her skin still twinkled like small electric lights, but burning now. "Weak, a burden, no mind of your own," Bob called her.

She tossed back her hair, but it made her dizzy, so she squatted beside David, pressing her cheek to his tummy. His smell was her salvation, binding her back to gravity. No dearer perfume than the fragrance of her own child!

"Do you want more children?" Mrs. St. George asked from on high.

Raising her head, "Oh yes," dutifully.

"How many?"

"At least two."

"Lachlan will make a good father, I'm sure."

If only he was there to father her, she would be happy. David would have to do, for the time being. She helped him hang a few more ornaments, then they both watched Mrs. St. George place the angel on the tip of the tree. She squeezed David's hand, and said a quick prayer. Let this feeling pass!

"Would you like a Bloody Mary," asked the woman. "Oh yes, fine!" Now her prayer had been answered. The new injection of alchohol took the edge off the rest, and her mood lifted, she felt brave. When Lachlan returned, alone, he and his mother retreated upstairs, giving Caralisa a chance to sneak a larger dose of vodka into her glass. When they returned, they produced a glittering sapphire and diamond ring, for Caralisa, now, to wear.

She looked into the blue and glittering lights of the ring, as into a great ocean which lapped and lapped with miraculous ease out of a blank horizon. The blessings coming her way overwhelmed her, and washed away the traces of suspicion and terror she usually knew. As she hugged Lachlan, she caught a glimpse of his mother's expression. She was looking at David with great dislike and irritation, as he fumbled with an ornament beside the tree.

*

The drive back from Boston was slow, nosing the car through the thick snow. The windshield wipers, batting in a rhythmic pattern, put David to sleep. Caralisa lounged against Lachlan who was musing on various philosophical questions for his sermon the next day.

I think I'll talk about marriage, he said, and connect it somehow to faith. That shouldn't be too hard. I've got a standard Christmas sermon but this week is special.

Because of us?

Because of us.

Will you come over tonight?

Of course!

But the snow.

I'll park at the end of your road.

Then I better wake David up, or he'll never go to sleep tonight. And that would be no good.

No good, he agreed rubbing his hand within her warm thighs.

Reluctantly she woke David and brought him into the front seat, where he fiddled with radio dials which made no music. Are we almost home? he kept asking. Almost, Lachlan kept saying. At their highway exit, David leaned back in Caralisa's lap and listened to the beat of the windshield wiper. It produced a chant from him. Elmer *Fudd*, Elmer *Fudd*, Elmer *Fudd*. Caralisa resisted pinching him, but turned scarlet.

Do you like Bugs Bunny too? Lachlan inquired.

I like Elmer the best, said David.

He is pretty funny.

Elmer Fudd. Elmer Fudd. Elmer –

Shh, warned Caralisa, we're almost home.

But he continued, whispering, the chant, until they came to the end of her road.

I better walk down, she told Lachlan, or else you'll get stuck.

Thanks, Dear Heart.

She took out her small bag and David leaped happily onto the

snow-thick earth, then ran to her mailbox to check out its contents for her. Lachlan drove off, the car weaving slightly on the
slick road. Caralisa snarled at David, took her mail and
threaded her way down the road, ahead of him.

Inside, she turned on the heat but stayed in her coat. There was a
bill and a letter from Bob, which she read, while David plunged
into his toys, glad to be home.

> Dear Caralisa,
>   I can certainly understand your desire to keep custody
> of David, but I'm afraid I'm going to fight it in court. Even
> if you were rolling in money, I would still say you are
> unable to be a proper mother for David, and I could prove
> it. Money is not the issue; neither is your having a career or
> not. It is your personality and your life style. You have
> never been able to take care of yourself, so how could you
> take care of a child?
>   I can prove, in court, that you have had a series of
> lovers, some of them drug addicts and anti-American
> types, and that you never cared if David knew it or not.
> What you do with your life is your business, but not what
> you do with David's life. Go ahead and get yourself a
> lawyer, but I plan to fight you all the way.
>   I'll pick David up around five on the 24th and hope
> you will have reached your decision by then.
>
>   Bob

> "Motherfucker! Asshole! Rat shit of the universe! Racist!
> Pig! Monkey piss! Shit-faced monument to male chauvinist
> pigdom! Animal slave! Bag of pus and blood! Fuck face!
> Fucking indigent slob! Hypocrite! Liar! Apple of the
> C.I.A.! Traitor! Turd! Motherfucking slave-driving
> asshole!"

Caralisa stood shouting, in her coat, in the center of the kitchen,
her face a mask of angst. David, hunched over his yellow truck,
paid no attention, but went on humming like a motor.

"Rotten pig. Sly genius. Filthy domineering piece of cat shit. Fascist. Nazi. Honky white-ass piss dumb fuck. I hate your balls! Stuff it up your ass. Cocky little shitface." She threw off her coat and marched into the bathroom; stripped; and plunged into the shower. Hot water poured over her naked skin.

"Take him then, you piss dumb fuck. Take him, I can't stop you, asshole, you get everything you want, I hate you. Knife-in-your-back. Shit hole. Slug. Worm. Business man."

She was crying, too, as she talked. Her contorted lips dripped water, and her hair.

"You're all a bunch of fucks. Rapists. Racists. Slobs. Pigs. Nuts. Take him. You can have him! He's all yours! I give up! You win! I lose! Shit! Take him!"

She stuck her bawling head out of the shower and shouted:

"You're going to live with Daddy!"

EIGHT

✳

You can always pretend there is an end to pain, but then the
Unavoidable rises. The Unavoidable is what it's all about, wow,
the rest is sucked away into oblivion. Every day, unavoidable,
every minute, an obstacle, the endless obligations and choices,
the ears pricked and neck switching from side to side. So high
you can't get around it. Wow! The Unavoidable. The dentist.
The doctor. The uterus. The school. The money. The law. The
car. How shall we sing the Lord's song in a strange land? By the
rivers of Babylon, there we sat down, wow, we wept, when we
remembered Zion! But Zion did not remember us, or how we
got here, or the Lord, now God, no god, did not remember us.
Blessed but not saved. Oh wow, the Unavoidable clangs in the
left ear, then the right, at noon, then six, the angelus, a shift in
light and tempo, but not an escape. You can go and go and call
yourself Free, but free you are not, of little troubles, or big,
coming down with clangs like harps from cold, old willows. The
earth is littered with strings, and jelly, Nature is not tidy. What a
life, Wow! Surely in vain the net is spread in the sight of any old
bird with eyes, can see the checkered cloth hanging in the trees
and will fly the other way. Surely but never, not clever enough to
avoid the thinner net, a veil strung across the willows like a
seaside mist, into which, it flies. Oh wow, I would lay down my
spirit at the feet of the Lord, I would be glad when they said let's
go into the house of the Lord, it's time. But my feet are standing
on the coals of juniper, sharp pavements of the mighty. And
what good does it do if I am for peace, if everyone else is for
war? If I am for spirit, and everyone else is for money? If I am for
freedom, and everyone else is for property? Wow, what good
does it do, if I am different and everyone else is the same?
Famine, poverty, drought will come into my house, if I am alone
and not the same. Wow, let's face it. The Unavoidable comes
into the house and sits down. Or you can go and go and it
follows you, at your side, then right ahead. Obligation, neces-
sity! The best moments are solitary, hallelujah, I'm a bum, wow,
really, a zap of happiness, for after intercourse every creature
sighs, is sad, but when alone you can cry Comforter! and it hears

you, it is your meditation through the day. You can lift your eyes up to the hills and get no help. You can turn them to the city and see lights, the princes of persecution have lanterns in their windows, and await you. But wow how I love to be alone! Solitude is a lamp unto my feet and a light unto my path. There are no hills in such darkness, but the sloppy effects of Nature's habits keep you tripping, even with a candle in your hand, and it comes again, soon as you venture out, with hope, the Unavoidable! Turn back, and you must speak with the enemies at the gate. My heart is in the highlands of Zion, where the water runs deep and black, and only silver bubbles glitter at the base of waterfalls, the rest is clean. And if I look too deep into its depth, I see the net they've set for me, floating there, not far beneath its surface beauty. Cadmium yellow is the sun. Yards of blue canvas is the sky. But when I grew hungry, and had to go home, the shadows were long across the winter grass. I looked to my right and looked to my left, but there was no one, no one cared for my soul, there was no Comforter but, wow, the knock of the Unavoidable on the small of my back, was almost comforting. Then it was almost kind. If I was alone, I had no wants, wanted nothing, and couldn't survive, wanting nothing. But, in company, I watched the others dash their little ones against the stones, and wow, it didn't make me happy. But what could I do? I had to admire them for wanting to live, which was more than I could say for myself, for even if the princes of persecution arrived, these others would survive by conversion, trickery, lies. They would bow down before the Unavoidable, they would fall into its nets. But I, alone, would be trampled, and then goodbye to my meditation! Goodbye to my black river in Zion! Goodbye to my glass hands and wooden skirt! Shattered! What use, then, is all this thinking? Far better to hoard dollars, make war, fuck, drink and own a home than to starve, staring, deep in thought, on the periphery.

✳

All day Saturday Kathy contemplated suicide. True contempla-
tion, a kind of meditation on the subject of her self. She was no
longer a virgin. That definition was gone. She wanted to die
with it. She lay on her bed transfixed by the attraction of the
grave's oblivion. Where the spirit of Father Steele would wel-
come her. She thought of pills, razors, and bullets. They raised
images of gore without sore sensations. Even as she closed her
eyes to imagine glutting herself with pills, she envisioned a sort
of video screen with bloody figures darting hither and thither,
knocking each other out. She held her breath for a very long
time. Red spots dimpled her inner eyelids. She gasped. Prayed.

There was a knock on the door to her room.
    It's Mom!
Jesus Christ, Kathy muttered. Come on in.
Her mother entered, looking frazzled, miserable, but still, to
Kathy, quite beautiful. She closed the door and leaned against it,
her expression lean and lonesome.
What's wrong? asked Kathy.
    I hate this life.
What happened now.
    The boys just broke the dial on the television, fighting over
    some dumb-ass show. Randy will kill me.
You?
    For letting it happen.
Kathy flopped back on her pillow, raging out a sigh. Her mother
drifted over, arms clasped across her thin waist, and hunched.
    What's wrong with you? she asked.
I hate myself.
    You did something. With that Elmer guy. I knew it, said
    Mom.
You knew it.
    He's no good. Why choose him for the first time?
Don't make it sound like it's his fault that I'm weak.
Mom sat on the edge of the bed, and rubbed her knees with the
palms of her hands.

You're not weak. It's only human to want to—you know, at your age.

Thanks. That's a big help. I'm only human.

Well? So? What's wrong with that?

I don't want to be only human.

It covers alot of ground, said Mom.

Then she began, unexpectedly, rambling over remembrances of times she and Kathy spent together. Before. Alone. What fun it was, how funny, when the dog threw up on the mailman's shoe, and when their car broke down on a road in Connecticut and they had to sleep in a small-town police station.

Remember? They brought us pizza.

They were nice.

Really. It always surprises me how there's always someone nice to help out when things go wrong.

You help people. I've seen you.

Not for years.

True, said Kathy, not for years.

Want to run away?

Mom had that excited tremble in her voice which Kathy recognized from days of yore. It was a talking laugh. The more silly she got, the more serious she was. Kathy sat up on her elbows, grinning.

Wow! Yeah. Let's go!

We can, you know. We're not prisoners, serving some sentence. We're free!

Where will we go? And money!

Where there's a way there's a will.

Tomorrow's Sunday. The banks are closed.

So we'll go Monday.

Your mood will wear off over the weekend.

Have I ever said this before?

No, but I know.

Then it's up to you, honey, to keep me strong.

As if I could!

You can. Have faith. I swear I'm serious.

Then don't get drunk tonight.

Kathy!

I'm not fooling. Liquor makes you weak.

Her Mom tossed her hair, little flush marks on her cheeks, as if she were shocked at the suggestion of her over-indulging. She pushed at her hair, with a glance in Kathy's mirror, and leaned on the doorknob.

Don't you drink, either, honey, if you're going out, and get yourself some pills. Soon. If this is going to be habitual.

Kathy groaned, Habitual?

I'm not criticising you!

She groaned again.

Well, just please plan our escape, okay?

When her mother was gone, Kathy lay flat with her eyes shut, watching those blood spots drift up and down like sparks on the Fourth of July. To be completely anonymous was her sole wish again, anonymous and alive. But her mother had disturbed the stillness of that climate, by raising her hopes of a change, of escape, and now she couldn't reach down into the gravity of that blissful space.

❄

Lachlan, at the rectory, had to fish around for an old sermon for the following day. He was hung over, and suffering, too, from a kind of nervous exhaustion succeeding his weekend at home. He slammed through the drawers of the desk, looking for the portfolio in which he contained his favorite sermons. Adele had fussed, putting everything away from him; he didn't know how to tell her that for him disorder was order. Now he was lost, and he cursed.

In the fourth drawer, he moved his hand around, blindly, and pulled out what he thought was his object. It wasn't. It was a large black notebook, unfamiliar. He opened it, horrified to imagine he had forgotten some part of his own past. What was this thing of his? He read:

Let my enemies smite me, too, who worked in the gins of inequity.
I know you Lord will maintain the cause of the afflicted and the poor. But what about the sailor on the ship of the wicked, who works in your name, as the wood cleaveth the water?
The arrogant and fulfilled go about like talebearers telling secrets, nodding and flattering.
To ward off boredom, I conjured images, vile, over her body.
Yes. Better is the sight of the eyes than the wandering of desire. Much better!
There are three kinds of healing: a charism, a gift and physical sacrifice. I ask now only to take on ALL the world's suffering, all of it, in the hope that you Lord will know what I mean.
I walked through the substance of my heart and discovered a great longing and lust and sought her out and she became temptation itself.
To be consciously evil is one terrible thing, but to be insane and lose morality's raison d'etre, worse yet. No one should suffer the loss of the good law's meaning, and thereby the fruits of toil.
Guilty, by reason of insanity!
Lucky the ones to whom evil comes only in sleep, and

illuminates equations for the day's progression after.
Time equals morality's pace squared!

Lachlan read these statements and more, and more, until his
head was sore on all sides. They were a rambling pot-pourri
from Psalms, he could see, but they were also like a grille on a
jail, a rusted gate set in a void, through which he peered with
terror. The script was nearly his, but not quite, and so he had to
conclude that he wrote these notes when he was very young, or
else they belonged to someone else. Father Steele, of course.

The confusion filled him with a moral frenzy. Outside the snow
was still falling, gentle white drops against the violet sky. It
thickened on the thinnest branches and an old leaf held some
like a spoon of sugar. Occasionally he glanced through the
window, at these graceful heaps, his vision blurring.

He sensed some great, perpetual failure in himself; it spread a
white glow over his whole past, a glow striped with the shadows
of a grille. And fretting there, over his evasion of commitment
and responsibility, he neglected to call Caralisa.

❄

She sat on the edge of David's bed. The snow ticked on the windowpanes, a branch scratched the glass. She was rubbing David's back to put him to sleep; the gesture was soothing to them both. Fatigued, and tense, simultaneously, the same words repeated themselves in her mind. She had called Bob, while still dripping wet, and shouted into the phone, Okay, Fuckface, you can have him. She heard him begin a cheery little speech of thanks, but bammed down the phone.

David was alarmed. He even cried and said he didn't want to go. She tried to blame it on him.

"But you said you hated Lachlan and wanted to live with Daddy. That's what you said."

He howled, I didn't mean it, and she howled, and said, Why didn't you say so? As if he had masterminded the whole scene! She didn't feel guilty, until he was in bed. Whenever he fell asleep, she felt guilty about him, anyway. But this time it was worse than usual. She was really angry at herself, and vowed she would rub his back every night until he left.

"Well, everyone's getting what they wanted, except me. Lachlan, his mother, and Fuckface. Lachlan probably lit a candle and prayed this would happen."

It was dark out. She wondered now, where Lachlan was. Usually the soul of promptitude, she could only imagine the worst. He had flown the coop, or else he had crashed in the snow. Without him, where would she be? Without David, too. She would be utterly alone in the world. She went into the kitchen and the clock said it was almost eight! Later than she thought! She felt as if she were changing color, turning deep blue, as she stood in that small shack, the snow closing down around her.

David called her name, and she hurried to him, torn between fury at his being awake still and relief at the sound of another human voice.

What do you want now, she said in a surly tone.
His silvery face was glinting petulence.
   I'm going to tell on you, he said.
   Please go back to sleep. What about.
   About Elmer. I saw his penis.
   You did not.
   I did too.
   When.
   In your bed. One morning.
   Liar.
   Not liar, I did.
   No, you didn't.
   I did too.
   Come on, David.
Her voice was whining in her own ears.
   I'm going to tell, he repeated.
   Who.
   Lachlan.
   You better not.
   I'm going to.
   I'll kill you.
She made a lurching move to which he did not respond.
   I really will. I'll never forgive you.
His head on the pillow lay placid as a pie.
   I'm your mother! she shrilled.
   I'm still going to tell.
   You're not acting like yourself. This isn't like you!
His shoulders twitched a nonchalant shrug.
   You're just like your father then.
She sat on his bed and started to cry. He stared at the nape of her
neck for a full minute, his expression growing opaque and far-
seeing. From his perspective the view through the neck of his
mother would be of snow on glass, then of trim forest trees.
   Please go to sleep, she begged in a blur.
He didn't respond, staring away, and she turned to look down
at him, to expose to him the drops on her face, to conjure pity,
mercy, forgiveness, love. But he only looked back at her with the
cold judgement of one for whom a covenant has been broken.
Permanently.

❄

Kathy, on her way downstairs to meet Elmer, decided not to tell her mother where she was going. She knew what her Mom would think, and enjoy thinking: sex. This was the last thing on her mind, for herself, and she dressed in her usual haphazard way. A loose polyester top, plastic knee-high boots, baggy pants. She felt like a gypsy this way, pretty and free.

    Yuk! You're wearing those again?

Her mother made a face, a glass of whiskey in her hand, resting on the kitchen counter. Kathy grabbed her coat and left before Elmer could ring or enter. She was cursing her Mom under her breath.

    Do I look ugly in these clothes? she asked him, throwing open her coat.

I don't notice what you wear, was his enigmatic reply, I'm hungry.

Kathy followed him up into the warmth of the van. The snow lay high and thick along the sides of the road. The only sounds that night were the sounds of snowplows rolling down the streets. Kathy hummed, aggressively, a hymn.

Well, said Elmer, you sound happy. Did I do that to you?

    No way. If I'm happy, it has nothing to do with you or anyone.

That's what I like to hear. Sit close, he said.

    She moved next to him, but not against.

Listen, I'm sorry, he said.

    For what?

You know. Last night.

    You wish you hadn't?

If you do.

    I don't care.

You really are cold-blooded, he said with the laugh in his voice.

    Well, it had to happen sometime.

It's just too bad I'm leaving so soon. I mean, after doing that to you. You know.

    Maybe I'll be leaving soon too.

Sing for me.
     All I know by heart are hymns. You'd hate them.
I won't listen to the words, just the melody.
She didn't sing the words, but hummed the tune of Amazing
Grace, while the van lumbered over the dense weights of fallen
snow.

✳

Lachlan banged the desk drawer shut, and slapped down an old sermon, which he picked and needled at for a few moments, incorporating a line from the page he had read earlier. "Better is the sight of the eyes than the wandering of desire."

And then he remembered Caralisa, waiting. Eight o'clock! He banged the palms of his hands down on the desk top and jumped to his feet.
　　What have I done now?
He grabbed the phone and called her.
　　I'm sorry. Forgive me.
　　You fell asleep?
　　No. I started reading and lost all track.
　　I'm just glad you're all right.
　　I'll be right over.
　　Drive slowly!
　　Do we have anything to eat?
　　Rice. Lettuce. Beans. Cheese.
　　Ah good. I can't wait.
　　But be careful, she said.
　　I will.
He smooched two kisses into the air and hung up. A glance out the window told him he was a fool to go out. At least he had snow tires, but if he got stuck, it would be a disaster. Climbing into his boots, he had a vision of himself trapped at Caralisa's shack for the whole night and having to walk back for the early service at dawn. If he ran through the vision fast, it wasn't too bad. But when he slowed it down, there was nothing but trouble. A struck car, whirring tires, empty highways and public exposure of his sex life.

His body heated at the mere mental mention of 'sex life' as he stepped into the icy blizzard. His face was struck as if by a wet mop. He bowed his head and hurried to his car. It moved, it inched along, and, for some inexplicable reason, his mind kept repeating the line "Better is the sight of the eyes than the wandering of desire."

❊

Caralisa's mood improved as soon as she got the call from Lachlan. She told herself she could survive anything as long as he was loving. And as if to reassure herself on this point, she drifted to David's room to see him sleeping. His sleep would indicate his ability to survive anything too.

The bed was empty. She switched on the light. She called his name then and moved around the house, looking in closets and under beds, her face growing red. When she found his boots and jacket gone, she stamped her foot and opened the outside door. The cold affronted her, she put on her coat.

Outside she saw no tracks, no signs, but called his name in a high voice and trudged through the fresh snow to her car. Her lungs swung weights, one rage, one fear, and she crawled inside the car and all around outside it, even looked in the trunk, but he wasn't there.

A cold astonishment grew in her, as if she were turning into a fold of snow. She didn't know what to do. She looked north, east, west, south and up at the moon trailing veils of limp clouds, no more snow. She marched around the house twice, calling his name. But the snowy feeling grew paralysing and stiffly she entered the house and poured herself some wine.

Her mind leaped from thought to thought, invisibility rushing under like water. He had run away. He would return; they always do. She had no choice but to sit and act debonnair, to talk to Lachlan as if nothing had happened. She shut David's bedroom door, went to the phone to call Lachlan and stop him from coming. Shame emblazoned her cheeks.

Lachlan had already gone. She stood stock still, unable to make a decision this way or that.

A rush to the door and she called into the cold, David, David!

You better come home or you're in deep trouble!

David! David! Please come in!

David! David! I love you! You can live with me!

I was only joking!

❋

Elmer and Kathy munched on french fries, Big Macs and frappes. MacDonalds was empty except for them—yellowed tables under the bright lights, and behind the counter, one girl serving; in the kitchen, a couple of boys. Kathy knew the girl, from school, so she insisted on sitting at the farthest table by a window.
    Incredible weather, she said.
Really. I hate it.
    But it's so pretty, and quiet.
Makes me nervous. Driving in it. And just being in it.
    Why?
It's stupid. Extra. Like too much. I don't know why they invented snow.
Elmer ate with his eyes lowered, and talked with his mouth full. He ate to fill up, not to savor, or linger over.
    What'll we do after? asked Kathy.
Take a walk in the snow.
    But I thought you hated it.
I figure, since I'm leaving, I might as well get to know it. You know.
    Lucky I wore boots.
Kathy, smearing and dashing ketchup all over her fries, eyed Elmer intensely. He raised his eyes, winked one at her, and lowered them again.
    Guess what, she said.
No, what.
    My Mom and I are—running away!
He went on chewing, gulped, and took a draught of his frappe, before responding.
Where, when and why?
    Monday. She just wants to get out. She's had it.
And you?
    I go where she goes. It's always been that way.
You don't sound too confident.
    What do you mean?
I don't know. You sound like you're faking.

I'm not! She told me she wanted to leave.

He looked at her face, carefully, then down: I believe that part, but I don't believe you believe her.

We'll see about that.

I hope it's true for your sake. You always talk about leaving. Like me.

Not quite. You're at home in the world.

Kathy gazed out the window, through her own reflection, and into the image of her mother, whiskey in hand, at home.

Don't look so sad, said Elmer.

I'm not.

I'll write to you. How's that?

Nothing.

Why not?

Because you won't, and it wouldn't matter if you did.

He touched her hand. She jumped it back. And they went on eating then in a silence as confirmed as sleep.

✳

Someone is parked at the end of the road, were Lachlan's first words on entering.

Who, said Caralisa sideways, teeth clenched.

A van. A new one. Might have gotten stuck.

A van?

You know. One of those big wagons. I can't stand them myself. Nobody came here?

No, she said and her blood cooled in her extremities, toes and fingers all at once numb. She turned her face away from his. He stamped the snow off his feet, removed his boots, threw his jacket down on a chair. The table was set for two. The smell of cooking warmed the room.

David asleep?

Sshh.

A rabbit without wit in a briar patch. Not Brer Rabbit, but some small brown creature strung up for the kill; Caralisa felt like this, and terror swamped her. Her fingers trembled. She knew it was Elmer's van; and now he had David. A conspiracy! Abduction!

I'm hungry, said Lachlan.

I hope it isn't a m-murderer.

Don't say that.

But maybe somebody's prowling around.

Not in this weather. They must have walked to the highway to get help.

She slung the food on the table without grace. Lachlan noted this and her pale face and poured them each a glass of wine, sitting down.

Ah, he sighed, I actually accomplished something this afternoon.

Caralisa did not respond. She could not believe what was happening and how it somehow made perfect sense. Wildly her mind conjured other forms of perfection: the perfect murder, the perfect idiot, the perfect insect, the perfect lie — perfect being what everything in the world was, after all. A perfect monster! A perfect rat! A perfect potato!

Yes, it felt good to do something well.

A perfect sermon?

Well, I wouldn't go that far, but certainly one of my best.

I'm not hungry.

You don't look well. What's wrong?

Nothing. I'm perfectly fine.

No, you're not. What's wrong, darling?

The word darling got to her, and her throat unlocked a quick sob.

I'm scared of that van, she said.

But I'm here to protect you.

Not for long.

Her wet eyes turned on him.

I'm upset, she said, because I agreed to give David to that shit. His father, I mean.

You did?

He stood up and went to her, putting his hands on her shoulders and leaning down.

Why?

You know why.

Because of me?

David. Doesn't like you.

Lachlan's hands dropped, he moved away, his expression alarmed.

Don't do it because of me, he said.

She leaped up and followed him anxiously saying no, no, no.

You're sure?

No, no, it's all right.

It wouldn't be a good way for us to start—with you resenting me.

I don't, I don't!

All right then. Give me a hug.

She tossed her arms around his waist, her head on his chest, and sobbed, Eat.

I'm not hungry anymore.

They stayed still, holding each other at the door to her bedroom. Her eyes were wide open, his were closed. She was praying that he would go, so she could figure out what to do about David.

Do you want to lie down? he asked.
Yes. But.
But what?
Then you'd better go. I think I just need to be alone.
But the van?
That's okay. I was just kidding. I'm not scared.
Well, all right, he said smoothly.

As he fingered her hair he had to admit to himself that he was anxious to leave. Not just the weather, but the event of her announcement about David. He wanted to think about it, to deal with the instantaneous guilt he felt at getting what he wanted—Caralisa free and simple. It was like winning the lottery, that blow of fortune as astonishing as a mistake.

But before I go, I want to be sure you are settled with your decision.

She untwined her arms and went to her bedroom with fingers trembling over a button. Head down, she considered going to David's room then and there, pretending to just discover him gone. But the image speeded up, its force impossible to handle.

I'm settled, no problem, she said to Lachlan behind her.
You're sure?
Perfectly positive, she insisted.
Well, I'm not leaving till you're all tucked in.

She would've liked to joke and frolic, imagined the activity with great yearning, but turned on the light and said, Tell me you love me.

I love you, he said obediently but with heart.

❄

They had seen Lachlan enter from their position in the pines. Kathy gasped at the air around her like a woman in labor. You like cold air? asked Elmer.

It's so dry! She squeezed her toes inside her boots. Besides, I'm a little shocked.

Just a little?

Alot of little.

They both looked up at the white and moon-lined branches above them.

You want to walk near the house?

Not really. I mean, I've seen.

You believe me now?

I already did.

I thought seeing was believing.

He turned his back and began to walk stiffly through the drifts with Kathy close behind him. She used his tracks, but fell from side to side, clasping at the trees for support. Elmer was looking up at the sky, his face damp and rosy, but knotted, too, as if grieving. Creamy trees extended deep around them, the tint of bones, crematorium ashes. He made his way behind the house where squares of yellow light drooped on the flossy snow, and turned to Kathy. She was hanging back.

I'm cold, she said.

I know. But come over here, and shh.

Look. Some little animal's been here before us!

She pointed at a mussy blue trail, and let her eyes follow it, because it had some significance to the thoughts she was thinking. They had to do with leaving marks, not getting away with murder, anything.

I don't think we should do this, she whispered, it's against the law!

Not yet. Not really.

I've seen all I need to see. He's not what I thought.

Nobody is, muttered Elmer. Come here.

She moved to his side, her eyes focussed on the snowy ground. Elmer knocked his boots together, his toes icy and glanced at

Kathy for a reading of her mood. The downturn of her face was striking to him, a lash out of the invisible.

Hey, Kathy, he whispered.

    Her response was a glance up.

Is this upsetting you?

She shrugged and looked around through the snowy trees towards the buried river.

Then come look.

She sighed outwards, frothy air, and they strained upwards, peering into Caralisa's room. A small lamp was lit by the bed. The bureau was heaped with colorful beads and earrings. Elmer recalled himself in there, her sham, his shame.

Look, he whispered urgently.

Lachlan and Caralisa entered, locked.

❉

Lachlan unbuttoned Caralisa's blouse and said he would give her a back rub. But she said, No, don't bother, you better go. He went to turn off the light.

Leave it on, she said.

Why?

I don't know. I'm nervous.

I can see that. But don't you have a shade?

He looked up the window.

I'll pull it down at least, he said.

And as he raised his arm to drawn down the shade, he peered out to see if the snow had stopped for good. Facing him were two faces.

Lord, he whispered and pulled down the shade.

His heart banged on his chest like snowballs on glass. He felt it might break, but turned around easefully to Caralisa.

I think I'll just stroll around the house to make sure no one is there.

No. Don't!

Their eyes fastened on each other. But Lachlan only saw what he had seen—white faces bleached against a blueish background. It was as if his deepest psychic fear was being realized. He was caught! In the act! And those faces, like angels even, had a familiar quality, recognizable features, as if he had been awaiting their arrival for years.

But you're so scared, he murmured, I think I just better check.

Caralisa, all jerks, grabbed a sweater and rolled it over her head, and on.

Let me come with you, she said, I'll just check on David.

You stay here. Do!

No, I'll come, she insisted, after I've taken a peek at David.

❄

Outside, Kathy was following the blue trail in the snow, away from Elmer's immobility, as if this were a deliberate plan laid out for her. Acres of dainty apple trees stood up with lace edging, across the invisible river. And walking through those icy filigrees, she was subsumed by a sensation of deep heat. It was anonymity at its best.

The blue trail was thick, wavering and wide. The presence of afterlife saturated the atmosphere, she couldn't say why, or why it was like the meeting of heat and cold, inner and outer. Several paces ahead, though, she saw a shape like a plaid hen on the open expanse of the hidden river.

Since it was moving, it was, to her mind, anxious, and she went forwards towards it. The wings of that hen were lifting up and to the sides, and the body was not feathered, but held a human face. Round, pale, and open like a chick to the chilly sky. She knew what was happening, and walked anyway over the water, ankle deep in the soft snow, to the boy, who was sinking and struggling not to; and she felt, under her, what she had, for some time, anticipated. A collapse in the shell of the earth, a crack in its surface. Not strong enough to hold her, or any child. It didn't surprise, or, therefore, scare her.

The cold water received her weight, but she kept her eyes focussed on the boy's face. She really wanted to save his life, seeing him as if he were she — a floating object with one emotion—hope, which made him worthy of the world. And she threw herself at him and hoisted him up, back onto the white shell, where he crawled, like an infant, and called his mother's name in bird-sized peeps, across the crumbling surface.

She gave him all her hope as one piece after another broke around her hands, and floated, then crumpled, sank, dissolved around the enormous weight of her wet body. Still warm, however, she watched Elmer's tall figure merge with the small one, leaning and lifting, and they broke off into the black and white branches she had left behind.

She floated and dropped, floated and dropped, deeper, in silence and black water, struggled a little, but had to give in, no choice, as if she had performed a task which had taken years of preparation, and which ended in unavoidable rest.

❉

Elmer forgot all about Kathy's existence in his rush to give David warmth. He held him tight against his chest and gasped, stumbling, towards the house, and now Lachlan, coming out. Lachlan slipped and staggered on a belt of concealed ice and landed against a tree.

Fool! said Elmer, What's going on?

Deliberately he shoved against Lachlan on his way to the door. Caralisa came out.

David!

He's frozen stiff. Half drowned. What's going on?

Elmer's face was wound up like a face in a tree, and Caralisa ran back inside.

Get him a blanket. I'll strip him down. He'll have to go to the hospital.

David was heavy-lidded, a pale spring green, and shivering his way towards sleep. Elmer undressed him near the fire, his own fingers shaking on the buttons, while Caralisa ripped apart the boy's bed.

You fool, Elmer said as Lachlan came in and over, his mouth ajar, stunned. You dumb-ass reverend fool. How did you let this happen? So busy looking for pussy? God damn.

Lachlan flushed hot: I don't know how he was out, got out. Is he all right?

Caralisa, give me the blankets quick.

She stuffed them into Elmer's arms and squatted beside David, her features stricken with sudden tics.

Oh honey, honey, honey, she sobbed.

Elmer acted efficiently, and his hands slowed down. A slow deep breathing began to fill his chest, and he wrapped David, fold by fold in layers of blankets, all the time looking at Lachlan.

You didn't know he was out? At night? You're really good for nothing, aren't you, Mr. Reverend Good-For-Nothing. Just a lump of clay. I wonder if you can even get it up when it comes down to it. Can you? Huh? No answer? Well, she'll tell me… Can he, Caralisa? Can he even get it up for you?

Shut up, Elmer, she sobbed, her hands flicking around the blankets and the boy's dazed face, And hurry!

 She wants me to shut up and hurry and I will. But you are some kind of fool, I've got to say it, to think you can go after pussy and not even get it up.

Elmer!

 I know her. She knows me. In the Biblical sense. Biblical. Ha. Get it? Biblical man?

Elmer lifted up David, a heavy load of skin, bone and blanket, and looked at Lachlan's disbelieving face, close up.

 Why would I lie? he asked. Tell me one reason why.

Elmer, come on.

 See? David knows me. So does she. But she really knows me. And how. Get it?

Caralisa shoved Elmer from behind, towards the door, her eyes averted from Lachlan. But he reached out and grabbed her arm before she got to the door.

 Is all this true? he asked, as if this question included the state of the universe. Is it true?

She started to say, We'll talk about it later, as this was her usual way, but his voice was like a chasm whose very drop made the facts imperative, and easier to throw out than evasions.

Yes! she cried, it's true, and ran after Elmer, out the door towards the van. She didn't stop running, till the engine was running, and she was inside.

Lachlan, alone in the house, sank hard on his knees beside the sofa, buried his face in his arms, and cried. He believed her. The sounds of his own sobs came to him as a dog's barking out through a closed window. The inner welter, a soundless mechanism, grief and disgust, was where his whole attention was fixed. Like wood cleaving water, his thoughts charged over the salt of his emotions, and made no more sense than the barking in his ears. No sense at all.

His hands tore at his hair, his torso moved restlessly, his knees knocked the floor, and his tears covered the wet cloth of David's pajamas. All he could see, as visual impression, was the woman lying, naked, under the other man, the stranger. Whoever she was, or he. And wherever, now, or why he must see them at all; who knew?

Sometimes, not often, an event occurs which so perfectly describes the fatal quality of a whole life lived, it is unmistakable and annihilating in its dimensions. Lachlan's comforts, all of them, flew away with the van into the snow. He watched them fly, and disperse, with his mind in tears, and when he seemed to be finished seeing them go, though he wasn't at all, he headed, red-eyed, home to his bed.

❄

In his bed Lachlan lay, held wide awake by the hope that he'd made a mistake. And when the sky whitened before the up-and-coming sun, he phoned Caralisa at home. She had not slept herself. Her voice was as alert as if it were noon.

Listen. David's okay, she said, but this is what's happening. Listen.

He did. She said she was delivering David to his father that morning, then going on, south, with Elmer. She was sorry, she said, for any pain she might be causing him, but she was obviously in no shape to get married.

And to a minister! Me? she added with a nervous laugh. I'll send back your ring.

He heard all she told him from his hunched position on the bedside, and stared out the window at what looked like a heap of silver poodles — dirty heaps of snow beside the Rectory walk. He found no words, not one, as a response, and laid the phone in its cradle, while his eyes stared at the world outside, waiting for him, with its obligations and disappointments intact.

❇

It was David who casually mentioned, to Elmer, that some lady saved him from drowning. They were driving in the direction of his father's home.

A lady? Elmer asked.

She was big, and she pushed me up. She fell down, said David.

An angel, I guess, it must have been, said Caralisa.

Elmer chilled around his neck and throat, and without turning to David, asked where the lady went.

In the water, the boy said.

Poor David! You've been through such a shock, his mother said, over her shoulder.

David frowned at his own face in the mirror.

Daddy will take good care of you, she added.

Until we come back and get you, said Elmer.

You promise you will?

Do I ever break my promises, asked Caralisa, do I?

David didn't answer, but lay out flat on the back seat, and watched the tips of the trees fly across the window, his arms folded on his chest. He wore an expression, both sad and frightened, identical to that which riveted Elmer's eyes on the road ahead.

❋

Lachlan did not perform the memorial service for Kathy. (Her body was found by a boy and a barking dog.) The new minister gave the homily and the eucharist; he was a roly poly fellow with a jolly but conservative air. All the classmates wept, listening to the hymns that Kathy sang.

And everyone, even the mother, guessed suicide, since it came so close on the heels of the other.

But Lachlan guessed otherwise.

He said nothing to anyone about the goings-on that night, and sat at the back of the church, his reputation intact. But on returning to Boston to work outside the church, and to live near his mother, he justified his silence, again and again, to another silence so large, he knew, now, he was not free but lost. There was a difference.

FICTION COLLECTIVE
Books in Print

Flatiron Book Distributors Inc., 175 Fifth Avenue (Suite 814), NYC 10010